THE COLONIAL TWINS OF VIRGINIA

Lucy Fitch Perkins

Republished Edition

THE
COLONIAL TWINS
OF VIRGINIA

By Lucy Fitch Perkins

ILLUSTRATED BY THE AUTHOR

Published by
Bluewater Publications
Printed in The United States of America

PREFACE

Long years ago, when this country was still an unbroken wilderness inhabited only by wild beasts and Indians, and rivers were the only highways of travel, there stood upon the southern shore of the swiftly flowing James a fine brick mansion belonging to Major George Burwell, a planter of old Virginia. His great estate of Honeywood stretched from the river-bank southward across many acres of cleared land deep into a virgin forest of immense cedars, pines, and water oaks. How far beyond the boundaries of Honeywood this forest extended no one then knew.

Toward the west, farther up the river, there were tobacco-fields, and farther still there were pastures for cattle. Nearer, in a hollow, a little village of log cabins provided quarters for the large colony of negro slaves belonging to the estate. Toward the east, beyond the home place, there were more farmlands, then forest again, with cart-paths leading to the plantation warehouses a mile and a half away, where a dock stretched far out into the deep channel of the James.

Along both shores of the river, like little kingdoms, lay other great estates — Brandon, Weyanoke, Westover — separated from one another by great stretches of forest and united only by rough trails winding beneath the trees, and by the great common highway of the yellow waters.

The unbroken forest which once stretched across the continent disappeared long ago, and where once stood Indian villages, great cities now lift their chimneys and their spires. Where once the only roads were dangerous forest paths, highways and railroads now weave a pattern across the length and breadth of the land, bringing the very ends of the earth nearer together than were adjoining plantations in that early day. Yet a little apart from its changed world the stately old mansion of Honeywood still stands among its ancient groves of cedar, water oaks, and pines, and still the muddy waters of the James flow swiftly by it to the sea. Still the yellow primroses border the garden paths which lead from the river-bank to its white-columned portico; still the mockingbirds and cardinals flit about its box hedges and fill the air with music; and still the happy voices of children wake the echoes, just as they did in the year 1676 when Tom and Beatrix Burwell lived there.

CONTENTS

I. A MAY DAY AT HONEYWOOD

One warm afternoon in a long-ago month of May, Tom and Beatrix Burwell sat at a low table in the pleasant school-room of Honeywood, writing the words "*Virtus omnia vincit*" in long rows in their copy-books. At a higher table near by sat their Scotch tutor, Mr. Alexander McNair. He too was writing, and for some time there was no sound in the room but the scratch-scratch of the three quill pens, and the buzzing of a huge fly which had sailed in through the open window and was trying desperately to fly out again through the glass. It was so still it seemed as if the whole world were asleep. Outside not a leaf stirred. Even the birds had sought the shadows, and only the cry of a jay or the harsh cawing of a crow broke the heavy silence.

There are many things any live, healthy boy of twelve would like better to do on a warm May afternoon than to sit in a school-room and write a Latin motto over and over again in his copy-book. "*Virtus omnia vincit,*" wrote Tom for the twentieth time, and the letters began to stagger down hill as if they were bound to fall in a heap in the lower right-hand corner of the page. He looked at them in disgust and ran his fingers through his tousled hair, leaving a smear of ink across his forehead. Then he wrote it twice more, and his pen sputtered and spattered drops of ink over the entire page! It was too much for Tom's temper. He threw down his quill, snorting with anger, and, seizing the ruined paper, tore it in two and flung the pieces on the floor!

Beatrix looked up from her work and said crossly, "Tom Burwell, stop jiggling. I can't write with you bumping around like that."

Tom cast a savage glance at his sister's copy-book. She was always the quicker one of the two, though her work was no better than his and her page was nearly finished. The sight of it exasperated him.

"I don't care if I do jiggle," he said furiously, and with that he took hold of the leg of the table and shook it on purpose!

Beatrix gave a little scream. "Oh, you bad boy!" she said, and Alexander McNair laid down his pen and gazed at them over his horn-rimmed spectacles like a surprised owl.

He was a tall man about forty years of age, with keen blue eyes behind his spectacles, and a heart much kinder than his grim face would have led one to expect. His face was at its very grimmest as he said sternly to Tom, with a Scotch burr in his speech that made his "r's" sound like a wheelbarrow rolling over a rough pavement, "Come her-r-r-e, my lad."

Tom rose sulkily and stood before him. "Tak' up those paper-r-r-s and hand them to me," said Alexander McNair.

Rebellion was written in every line of Tom's hunched-up shoulders as he stooped, but he lifted the crumpled scraps and laid them on the table. Alexander McNair slowly straightened them out, looked at the drunken letters and the ink smears, and then smiled quizzically at Tom. He was a man of few words as a rule, but those few were apt to be very much to the point.

"Happen ye can tell me what this word means?" he said, laying his finger on "*virtus,*" and looking at Tom over his spectacles.

Tom knew perfectly well what the whole sentence meant. It was the motto of the ancient House of Burwell, and ever since he could remember it had been inscribed above their coat of arms on the chimney-piece in the drawing-room of Honeywood. Over and over again, when the Twins were very small, their father had lifted them up so they could point with their little fat fingers at "round o" and "crooked s," and he had also taught them the words and their meaning almost as soon as they could talk at all.

"'Virtus' means courage," said Tom, looking very uncomfortable, for he saw a moral was on the way. Mr. McNair pointed to "vincit" and then to "omnia." "Conquers all things," translated Tom.

"Ah, weel," remarked Mr. McNair with some scorn, "Gin courage is sae michty, I'm thinkin' ye could give it a try at your-r-r task and your-r temper! 'Twould be a prood boast for auld Nickie, noo, if he could put down the son and heir of the House of Burwell with nae fiercer weapon than ane poor quill plucked from the feathers of an auld goosie!" As he made this speech, he looked very severe and his "r's" rumbled like distant thunder.

Tom flushed angrily, and across the table Trix visibly bristled. Though she and Tom were often what Tom called "brittle" toward each other, they stood staunchly together against the world when fault was found with either one. For an instant the angry boy and his tutor looked each other steadily in the eye, then Tom saluted stiffly, and, going back to his seat, took out another piece of paper, chose a new pen, and settled doggedly to the task of doing his lesson over again.

Alexander McNair watched him shrewdly, as he worked away with his nose almost touching the paper and his fingers cramped upon the quill as if it were a weapon and he were about to charge with it upon the bristling lines of letters now standing up right across the page like soldiers in a row. Beatrix, meanwhile, having finished her work for the day, rose to lay her copy-book on Mr. McNair's desk. As she passed Tom, she gave him a sympathetic pat on the shoulder and whispered these two words in his ear — "Big Oak."

Tom nodded without looking up, and Trix left the school-room. On the steps outside, patiently waiting for her, she found their faithful dog, Duke, and the two wandered off together. The words "Big Oak" had a secret meaning to the Twins. There was a great tree on the river-bank at some distance from the house which they had taken as their secret refuge and trysting-place. It stood, a gigantic mound of green, on a little point of land which extended far enough into the river so that one could look from it either down-stream toward the settlement of Jamestown, or westward toward the plantations further up the river.

High up in this tree Tom and Trix had built themselves a little house out of boards which they had brought one by one with great secrecy from their father's sawmill back in the woods. Not a soul but themselves knew of its existence. Here in a hollow of a great limb, safe from rain, they kept two books, which they had quietly borrowed from their father's small library of precious volumes.

One was Malory's "Mort d'Arthur," full of stories of brave knights and beautiful ladies, the other was Shakespeare's "Tempest." Besides these two books they had safely hidden among the branches two spears, whittled from soft pine by Tom, and two wooden shields which he had also made and upon which Trix had drawn their coat of arms in charcoal, with the motto on it just as it appeared on the chimney-piece at home. Here for days together, they played at life on a desert island, or enacted dramas from the history of Arthur's Knights, without fear of being seen.

When Trix left the school-house, she and the dog turned their steps toward the kitchen, which was in a separate building joined to the main house by a long, low corridor, just as the school-house was on the other side. Standing in the kitchen door as they approached was Mammy Jinny, the fat cook of Honeywood, holding in her hand a pitcher and a glass, and before Mammy stood her son, a black boy about the Twins' own age.

"Heah, you, Solly," Mammy Jinny was saying, "whar you done been? When I doesn't want you, thar you is, and when I does want you, whar is you? Ketch a holt of this yer pitcher and take it to Mars George. He's settin' on the porch with Miss Cynthy. Keerful now, and don' you spill ary drap."

As Solly departed, grinning, Mammy caught sight of Trix. She had been the Twins' nurse until they were too old to need one, and loved them still with complete devotion.

"Thar's ma chile," she cried delightedly, "come to see her ole Mammy! What you projickin round fer, honey?"

"Mammy," said Beatrix plaintively, "Tom and I are hungry."

"I lay you is," said Mammy, "an' Mars George he say he want supper late, account of he jes' come in from ridin' roun' the field hisself. He say he all cussed out and mighty tired and he want to tarry a spell before he set out fer to pacify his stummick."

"Well, then, Mammy," coaxed Trix, "give us a bite of something right now — just to keep us from starving."

"Sho' I will, chile," cried Mammy, and away she waddled to the pantry, from which she emerged a moment later bearing two huge pieces of corn bread spread with honey and wrapped in a white linen

5

napkin. Beatrix took the package, gave Mammy a hug which left her beaming, and, followed by Duke, quietly drifted out of sight along a cart-path which ran along the edge of the tobacco-field and lost itself in the woods beyond.

Past the field dotted with the gay turbans of the sweating slaves, past Adam Philpott, the overseer, on his big black horse, watching the negroes to see that they kept at work, past the overgrown negro graveyard where some of their number had been buried, she went, and then turned in among the shadows of the cedars, and, making a wide detour, approached their secret lair with all the stealth of an Indian on the war-path. When she reached the shelter of the great green tent, she tucked up her long skirts, took the packet of corn bread in her teeth, and, swinging herself up to one of the lower limbs, disappeared among the green boughs.

Once safely hidden in this leafy retreat, Trix proceeded to make herself comfortable. She reached in to the hollow limb and drew out the copy of "The Tempest," which she especially loved because it had a desert island and plenty of magic in it, then seated herself on the edge of the platform with her feet hanging over, and, placing the corn bread within easy reach, began to read.

Books were very scarce indeed in that far-away time, for Sir William Berkeley, the Governor, would not allow a printing-press in the colony, and all books had to be brought over in ships from England. Major Burwell loved good reading almost as much as he loved good horses and an outdoor life, and the library of Honeywood was one of his chief delights. There were no children's books in it, so Tom and Beatrix read the tales of chivalry and the comedies of Shakespeare until they knew them almost by heart. Beatrix had finished her corn bread and was deep in the story of Prospero and Miranda, when she heard a joyful bark from Duke and the soft sound of footfalls in the grass below. She leaned forward and, peering through the thick screen of leaves, caught a glimpse of Tom's brown hair and upturned nose below. In another moment he was seated beside her with his mouth full of corn bread and honey.

"Sandy didn't keep you long, did he?" said Beatrix. Sandy was their private nickname for Mr. Alexander McNair.

"He didn't keep me at all. I kept myself," Tom answered proudly.

"I know," said Beatrix sympathetically. "It's lots better to do things yourself like a gentleman, than to be made to do them, as if you were a slave, but sometimes you just have to obey! And, Tom, do you know? Sometimes I think it's almost as much of a nuisance to have to behave like gentlemen and ladies as it is to be made to do things."

"You don't have to behave like more than one," mumbled Tom, through the corn bread.

"Now, Tom, don't be silly," said Beatrix, leaning her chin pensively on her hand. "You don't know how desperate I am! Truly, I wish sometimes I didn't have to be a lady when I grow up, and have lots of manners and everything like that. Aunt Cynthia says I'm almost a young lady now and should be dressing up and going to dances and taking care of my complexion! She says I shouldn't always be running about with you and doing the things you do. She wants me to stay in the house and put up my hair like hers and learn to embroider the way she does. She says I act more like a boy than like the only daughter of the Burwells!"

"Well, don't you?" asked Tom. He laughed unfeelingly.

"It's all very well for you to laugh, Tom Burwell," Trix went on bitterly. "*You* don't have to look forward to giving up all the things you like to do and sitting around for the rest of your life all dressed up and embroidering horrid green parrots on footstool-covers! Tom, I just hate it. I want adventures — and to do things myself!"

Tom sobered down and looked grave at this desperate picture of his sister's future. "Oh, maybe it won't be so bad as all that," was all he could find to say to comfort her.

But Beatrix was well launched on a tide of grievances and did not mean to be rescued yet awhile. "Besides," she went on plaintively, "think of Rosalind and Celia in the Forest of Arden, and Miranda on the magic island! They had adventures enough, even if they were ladies!"

"I don't think much of their adventures," said Tom loftily. "They never did any fighting."

"No-o," Beatrix reluctantly admitted, "but exciting things happened and they were in them just the same. At least," she qualified, "they happened to all the beautiful ones. All ladies must have been beautiful in those days or else the ugly ones didn't count." This thought evidently disturbed her, for she swung suddenly round on her perch and said, anxiously, "Tom, do you think I'm a beauteous damsel?"

Tom considered her critically with his head on one side. "Well, I don't know," he answered at last. "Your mouth is a little too big, and your nose turns up some, but you have nice curls and Aunt Cynthia says you'd have a complexion if you'd only take care of it. I guess you're beauteous enough to have things happen to you, if that's all."

Trix looked relieved. "I think I'd rather be Rosalind than Miranda," said she after a pause. "It must have been fun to dress up like a man and live in the Forest of Arden. Wouldn't you like to live 'under the greenwood tree' all the time, Tom?"

"Snakes," said Tom, practically, "and rain, and snow, no beds, and mosquitoes." He slapped one viciously that was at that moment biting his leg.

At the word "snakes" Beatrix tumbled out of her romantic dream. "Ye-es," she quavered (she was afraid of snakes), "of course, it would be like that around here, but I'm sure it never rained and there were no snakes in the Forest of Arden."

Tom took out a large knife which he carried in his belt and began to whittle a stick. Trix leaned back against a friendly oak branch, opened her book, and was soon lost in her dream world again, and for a while there was no sound but the soft strokes of Tom's knife and the whistle of a cardinal down by the river. Then a breeze sprang up, making the leaves rustle and dance about them, and the water of the river lapped more loudly on the banks below, for the wind and the tide were both rising.

Beatrix sighed and closed her book. "I just love Honeywood," she said. "It's the sweetest, dearest place in the world. And I love Father a lot, and Aunt Cynthia — some, — and I love Mammy. Sandy is a dear, even if he is a horrid old Puritan and a Roundhead. One has to love people, and there aren't any other people here to love except the slaves, and of course they don't count. I simply can't abide that horrid Adam Philpott. I'm afraid of him. I heard Father tell Aunt Cynthia once that he was a convict before he came here, and once I saw a red mark in his hand." She leaned forward and whispered in Tom's ear, — and her eyes were wide with horror, — "Do you know, Tom, I believe he was branded on the hand with a hot iron when he was in prison!"

"Huh!" said Tom loftily, "I knew that long ago. But Father says he thinks old Pillbox is honest enough now. You can't get a gentleman for an overseer and a slave-driver. He's better than most, and, anyway, he's the best we can do."

Beatrix put her book carefully back into its hiding-place. "Well," she sighed, "even if it is dear and lovely, Honeywood is just as stupid as

Prospero's island before the shipwreck. All the days are alike — lessons, and Aunt Cynthia, and grown-up company from the other plantations for dinner. I just wish something exciting would happen."

II. THE NUNQUAM DORMIO OF BOSTON

At the very moment Beatrix said these words, a gust of wind from the river blew aside a bough of the Big Oak, and she caught a glimpse of the river through the leaves.

"Tom, Tom," she screamed, "maybe something is going to happen after all! There's a ship down the river!"

"Where?" cried Tom, leaping up so suddenly that the floor of the tree house swayed alarmingly.

"There!" said Beatrix, pointing toward the east, but the great boughs had already swung back and they saw only a mass of green leaves bobbing about in the breeze.

Ships were rare visitors on the James, and in their eagerness the Twins scrambled down out of the tree like a pair of squirrels and dashed to the eastern side of the knoll, where they could get a good

view of the river. Truly there was a ship, its canvas spread to the favoring breeze, sailing upstream toward Honeywood! It was still so far away they could tell nothing about it except that it flew the British flag, and, bursting with the news, they flew over the neck of the little peninsula and, casting their usual secrecy to the winds, ran straight toward the house, with Duke barking wildly behind them.

When they arrived, breathless and steaming, at the porch of Honeywood, they found their father still there, with Aunt Cynthia seated beside him calmly embroidering a green parrot on a square of coarse canvas just as Beatrix had said! At her feet squatted Solly slowly waving a turkey-feather fan to and fro to keep away flies and mosquitoes. Aunt Cynthia cast a look at her brother as the children came tearing toward the house, which said as plainly as words, "There, what did I tell you?" and before they could catch their breath to tell the news, she found time to say reprovingly to Trix, "My dear! How very unladylike! Your face is scarlet!"

Tom broke all the rules of good manners and interrupted her. "Father," he gasped, "there's a ship coming up the river from Jamestown!"

The words were no sooner out of his mouth than Major Burwell sprang up, clapped on his wig, which he had taken off and hung on the back of his chair because of the heat, and started at a great pace for the pier in front of the house, with the children trotting beside him. Even Aunt Cynthia was stirred.

"A ship!" she cried to nobody in particular. "Then likely there'll be company for supper! Solly, run and tell Mammy Jinny to prepare for guests!"

When he had disappeared on this errand, she put away her embroidery-frame, smoothed her hair, adjusted her skirts neatly, and followed her brother and the Twins at a sedate pace down the primrose-bordered garden paths to the landing-place. The news carried by Solly had spread like wild-fire, and by the time Aunt Cynthia had finished her preparations and made a stately progress to the dock, she found half the inhabitants of Honeywood there before her.

On the end of the pier stood Major Burwell, his wig awry and his face purple with heat, gazing eagerly down-stream. Beside him were the Twins, dancing with excitement, while Duke, quite bewildered by all the unusual stir, barked and whined at their heels. Near them Alexander McNair, his short, round locks blowing wildly in the breeze, peered eagerly through his spectacles at the ship, which seemed to grow larger and larger as it drew near.

A little apart from this group stood Adam Philpott, the overseer, and back of him a crowd of black house servants and field hands pressed forward as far as they dared, their white teeth gleaming and their eyes rolling with enjoyment of the unusual spectacle.

Nearer and nearer, like a gigantic bird, came the white-sailed visitor, its flag flying gallantly from the mast-head, and its sails bellying in the breeze. Though the river was navigable for ocean vessels for quite a distance up-stream, they came above Jamestown only to bring goods ordered by the planters, or to pick up cargoes of lumber or other heavy merchandise to carry back to the mother country. Such ships were the only carriers between the Old World and the New, and there would surely be news of England, letters from friends, books, fine clothes, and good things to eat and drink on the white-winged messenger now sailing so majestically up the river. To see it was to see dreams come true and hopes long-deferred fulfilled. No wonder every heart beat high with anticipation. Only to the slaves it brought no hopes, no dreams. To them it had only the excitement of a great spectacle, a moment's holiday in the weary round of their lives.

"It's Captain Pepperell's ship; I know it is," shouted Tom. "I can tell by the shape!"

At last the ship was near enough so Tom's sharp eyes could read the name. "It is, — it is!" he cried, "I knew it. There's her name, 'Nunquam Dormio of Boston,' on the bow!" He was enough of a Latin scholar to know that "Nunquam Dormio" meant "I never sleep," and, seizing Trix and spinning her round in an excess of delight, he cried, "It's truly Captain Pepperell's ship, — old, 'I never sleep,' — and the Captain himself will surely stay with us for supper!"

Captain Pepperell was an old friend of the Burwells. His ship made two voyages to England and back every summer, and it was upon him that they chiefly depended for all communication with their friends in the Old World. They could now see the sailors running about like busy ants, pulling at ropes and taking in sail; and on the poop deck, giving orders to the man at the wheel, loomed the familiar face of Captain Pepperell himself. At his side stood a smaller figure, dressed smartly in black, with white ruffles at neck and wrist.

"Look! That must be a passenger," cried Tom, plucking at his father's sleeve and pointing to the boy. "Oh, Father, do you suppose it's any one coming here?"

Major Burwell did not reply, but Trix, glancing up at his face, saw that it was as puzzled as her own and Tom's.

A great roar of cheers and shouts from the pier welcomed the Nunquam Dormio as she furled the sails and, dropping anchor in midstream, lowered a small boat. Then there was a breathless silence, as two sailors scrambled down the "Jacob's ladder," took their places on the rowing-benches, and, seizing the oars, kept the tossing little craft steady while two large boxes and several smaller ones were lowered into it. Then Captain Daniel Pepperell and the stranger climbed down the swaying ladder, and took their places at the stern.

"He is coming here! He is coming here!" cried Trix, squeezing her father's hand. "Oh, Father, who can he be?"

"Beatrix, my child," said Aunt Cynthia's warning voice, "restrain yourself," but Beatrix was too intent on the boat which was now nearing the pier even to hear her aunt's chiding voice.

Captain Pepperell, his brown face wreathed in smiles, was now waving his cap and roaring greetings to his old friend Major Burwell, and the boy, following his example, waved his hand and smiled up at the group on the pier. When the boat at last reached the landing-place, Major Burwell's hand grasped the Captain's while he was still on the short ladder by which they scaled the dock, and the boy was seized and helped ashore by Tom. Then the three children stood for a moment smiling shyly at each other, while Captain Pepperell formally greeted his old friends, and the sailors hoisted the boxes to the dock. The stranger was a handsome lad about the Twins' own age, or a little older, whose clothes of modish cut, ruffles of fine Flemish lace, and flowing hair, told them that he was no Puritan, but a young English aristocrat of Cavalier birth like the Twins themselves.

The moment he had finished paying his respects to the master and mistress of Honeywood, Captain Pepperell turned, and, laying his hand on the boy's shoulder, said, "I need hardly introduce your young kinsman, Archie Russell. You were doubtless excepting him," then,

seeing the blank look on every face, — he added, "Surely, Major Burwell, you know of the death of your sister, Lady Charlotte Russell of Kenmore, six months ago, and that she left her son to your guardianship?"

"Charlotte! Dead!" cried Aunt Cynthia. For an instant she stood quite still, stunned by the news, but when Archie stepped forward dutifully to kiss her hand, she put her arms about him and kissed him on both cheeks instead.

"How could we know?" said Major Burwell to the Captain when Archie had been warmly welcomed and there was time for explanations. "We have had no word. Not a ship has come up the river for months. It is years since we last saw my sister, and we had never seen her son."

It was now Captain Pepperell's turn to be surprised. "The Raleigh was due here at least a month ago," he said, "and Archie tells me she carried letters to you and also some silver plate and family heirlooms. I hope she has not met with foul play, but this coast swarms with pirates. They gave us a run off the Bermudas coming over, but by the mercy of God we gave them the slip, and here we are safe and sound." The Captain shook his head and sighed. "The Raleigh was a staunch craft," he said, "and her captain is a skillful sailor, but one needs the courage of a David and the cunning of the devil himself to outwit the pirates that infest these waters. They'll be the destruction of our commerce if they are not checked."

Major Burwell looked grave. Aunt Cynthia shuddered, and the Twins gazed in open admiration at the children and Archie, who had braved so many perils. Then Archie spoke.

"There was a portrait of my mother on the Raleigh," he said, "and the sword my father bequeathed to me." His voice choked. "Mother sent letters to you by the Raleigh telling you of my father's death and her own illness and asking you to be my guardian if she should die. She lived only a short time after the ship sailed. You see, sir," he went on, turning to the Major, "Mother wanted me to go to you because Kenmore now belongs to my half-brother Henry. He is the eldest son and came of age just before Mother died. There wasn't anything for me, you see, so Mother thought I would do better in the Colonies. She said she was sure you and Aunt Cynthia would look after me."

16

"And so we will, so we will," cried the Major heartily, patting Archie on the shoulder. Then, turning the boy's face toward the crowd of slaves still waiting on the pier, he said solemnly, "This is my dead sister's son, Archie Russell, once of Kenmore, England, now of Honeywood in His Majesty's Colony of Virginia, and henceforth to be treated as my own son."

Archie had never seen so many negroes in all his life before, but he smiled at the black faces before him, and was answered by a battery of friendly grins.

"Now get back to your work, all of you," shouted the master, "and you, Mammy Jinny, get a good supper on the table as soon as you can. Our guests must be perishing of hunger."

The crowd of field hands instantly melted away, with the overseer at their heels. The house servants disappeared behind the box hedges, and in a few moments there was no one left on the pier but the family and the Captain. Then Aunt Cynthia lifted her skirts daintily and led the way back through the primrose-bordered paths toward the open door of Honeywood. The Captain and the Major followed, but when they reached the white-columned portico, the children and their new-found cousin were nowhere to be seen. They had slipped quietly behind the box hedges, and Tom and Beatrix were at that moment engaged in taking Archie on a tour about his new home.

They showed him the stables, and the quarters, and the horses and dogs. They peeped in at the kitchen and called in the school-room on Alexander McNair, whose blue eyes lighted with pleasure at the prospect of so promising a new pupil. When, an hour later, they appeared again on the portico, they found Aunt Cynthia waiting for them.

"Where in the world have you been?" she said. "It's time to dress for dinner."

Trix at once started up the broad stairway to her room. Tom followed her three steps at a time and overtook her on the landing, and for a moment the two held a whispered conference.

"Well, Sis," said Tom, "something did happen at Honeywood after all, didn't it?"

"Oh, Tom!" said Beatrix clasping her hands and looking down over the carved banisters at Archie in the hall below, "it's just like Ferdinand coming to the magic island! Only it wasn't exactly a shipwreck that brought him! But it was just as good! I think Archie's splendid, don't you?"

"Don't know yet," said Tom warily. "Wait and see."

"Beatrix," came Aunt Cynthia's voice from the upper hall, "you'll be late for supper."

Tom instantly fled down-stairs to join Archie, and Trix ran upstairs to her room, where Pam, her maid, was already laying out her fresh clothes.

III. A DINNER-PARTY

While Tom scrubbed his face until it shone, and otherwise prepared to dazzle the guests with his appearance, Trix, under the hands of her black maid, Pam, was also undergoing a great change. Her hair was arranged in most distracting curls, which fell from under a coquettish cap, and her flowered gown was looped up at the sides over a petticoat of white satin. On her little feet were white satin shoes, which pinched her toes dreadfully, for she had been growing like a weed since the last load of finery had been received from England and her best slippers were now too tight.

When at last she crept gingerly down the stairs, holding to the banister-rail to ease the weight of her suffering feet, she found the family gathered in the great dining-hall below. Aunt Cynthia, very majestic in black silk and lace, was casting a critical eye upon the table service; Major Burwell and the Captain were whetting their appetites by a drink of spirits at the sideboard; and Tom, very splendid in his best

clothes, was showing Archie a picture of a horse which had been bred at Honeywood, and had won a race over a mare belonging to Governor Berkeley himself.

In the kitchen at that moment, things were much more lively. Mammy Jinny, her black face shining like polished ebony and her turban towering like a knight's helmet in battle, was gathering her forces for the serving of a supper that would fitly celebrate "Mars' Archie's" arrival in his new home.

Before the flames in the huge fireplace a wild turkey was roasting, and Solly, sitting on a low stool beside it, was unwillingly turning the spit so it would brown evenly on both sides. It had been cooking for a long time in a bake-oven and was now being given a golden crust before the leaping flames. On a pan over the coals a fish was cooking, and in a huge copper kettle set in a framework of brick a ham boiled merrily. There was golden corn bread baking in pans set in the hot ashes, and there were potatoes cooked in cream and kept warm over the steaming copper kettle. Oh the good smells there were in that kitchen! Far away from the main house though it was, savory gusts floated through the long corridor and were wafted into the dining-hall as the doors swung to and fro to admit the procession of slaves bringing the food to the table. Even Archie could not forbear a hungry sniff as the good things began to arrive, and as for Tom — he openly caressed his stomach and ogled the great pewter covers as they were brought in.

Archie's chair was placed between Tom and Trix, the Captain sat at Aunt Cynthia's right, and Alexander McNair, in his best flowered waistcoat, sat next to the Major. When grace had been said, and the food was served, Major Burwell turned to the Captain.

"It's a brave man that follows your calling, Captain Pepperell," said he. "I count myself no coward, but on your voyages you must look death in the eye every day. I wonder that so many men choose to follow the sea."

"We are caught young," said the Captain with a twinkle in his eye. "I made my first voyage from Boston to Plymouth with old Captain Saunders, of the Lucy Ann of Marblehead, when I was the age of these lads here. Captain Saunders was a staunch old sea dog and did a carrying trade along the coast for years. I caught the sea fever from him. My family wanted me to be a minister, and I took well to learning, but the sea called me and I had to go."

"Have you ever regretted it?" asked Aunt Cynthia.

The Captain was wrestling with a turkey bone at the moment and could not reply. There were no forks in those days, and every one ate with his fingers and his knife. Having got the better of the bone, the Captain wiped his fingers on his napkin and said, "Nay, Madam, 'the sea is the Lord's and he made it.' The Bible says so, and I am not one to criticize his handiwork. It's only the work of man and the devil that I find fault with."

"The Bible says the Lord made man too, doesn't it?" said the Major.

"It does," admitted the Captain, "and I'm not disputing it, but it's the devil that makes pirates out of 'em. They are fiends in human shape, and they infest this coast like rats in a corn-bin. It's likely they are the reason there have been so few ships in the James of late. It's on my mind that they've overhauled the Raleigh."

"This is a treacherous coast," sighed the Major. "It is full of inlets and bays that made good hiding-places for buccaneers, and our neighbors to the south are none too particular. They trade with the pirates right along because they can often get better prices for their goods from them than they can from honest men."

"That's the truth," agreed the Captain, "and our old mother England must bear a goodly share of the blame for it. She won't allow us here in the Colonies to trade with any country but England. You know how it is yourself, Major. You grow more tobacco now here in Virginia than England can use. She won't allow you to sell it to any other country, so you have to sell it to her at her own figure or else let your crops rot. She buys it at a low price and sells it to Holland at a high one." The Captain was plainly getting excited. "I tell you, sir," he said, thumping the table with his fist so that the glasses jingled, "the Navigation Laws are unjust. They are breeding trouble every day. What happens with tobacco happens with every other product of this country. I needn't tell you this. You must suffer from it like every one else."

Aunt Cynthia looked severely at the Captain. "Do I understand, sir," said she, her voice trembling with indignation, "that you uphold those who trade with pirates and criticize his gracious majesty's government? Indeed, sir, this smacks of treason!"

"Nay, nay, sister," interrupted the Major. "The Captain speaks but the truth. Hear him out. His is as loyal to the King — God bless him — as we are!"

Aunt Cynthia drew her lips tight together and said no more, though she looked volumes.

"You see, Madam," said the Captain, "it's like this. A man has a cargo of lumber all ready to sell. He could sell it to Holland or France for a good price. But England says, 'No, you can send it only to England and only in English ships.' Along comes one of these 'Brethren of the Coast.' He can trade anywhere in the world. He goes where he can get the best prices. He offers more money for the goods, and if the owner doesn't want to sell he'll take them anyway and shoot him into the bargain, as like as not. It's not in human nature to refuse an advantageous offer on such terms," said the Captain.

Aunt Cynthia sniffed. "The duty of a loyal subject is plain," said she. "Are we to be obedient only when it is to our advantage to be so? Truly, a strange doctrine to be preached in a loyal household!"

Major Burwell tried to lead the conversation into safe channels. "What cargo are you taking back with you this trip, Captain?" he asked. "I have a lot of lumber and game-pelts, beside quantities of pitch, waiting for you in my warehouses down below."

"What don't you wait and see if some pirate won't make you a better offer?" interposed Aunt Cynthia icily. The Major and the Captain ignored this thrust.

"I'm going farther up the river to Westover and Weyanoke and Brandon," said the Captain. "It will take a little time to pick up their produce and take their orders for England, but I'll be back in a few days for your cargo."

Alexander McNair had sat silently enjoying his dessert of nuts and raisins and saying no more than the children themselves, but it was not in reason to ask any Scotchman to listen to an argument without getting into it.

"An ye'll per-r-mit me a wor-rd," he said deferentially, "I'll say I'm minded of the fable of Æsop about the damie who killed the goose who laid the golden egg. The Colonies are the goose of old England, and their pr-roducts are the eggs. 'Twere well for her own interests if she minded the mor-ral of that tale."

Aunt Cynthia here looked so alarming that the Major thought best to treat this as a joke. He laughed heartily, then, rising, lifted his wineglass and said, "To the King — God bless him!" The others instantly rose, and lifting their glasses, drank the toast standing.

Aunt Cynthia did not seat herself again. Instead she said coldly: "Beatrix and I will leave you gentlemen to discuss these matters over your wine. They are undoubtedly too weighty for mere females," and, sweeping them a curtsey, she sailed majestically into the drawing-room, followed unwillingly by Beatrix. The men remained politely standing until the two disappeared through the door, then they seated themselves once more and the discussion began all over again. Tom and Archie took the privilege of their sex and remained to listen.

"I agree with you, Captain," said the Major. "The Navigation Laws need changing, but I believe in improving things from the inside, not from the outside. You Puritans didn't like the established Church, so you broke away altogether and set up a Church of your own, and I don't see that you are so much better than the rest of us after all! Who knows but you might have done us a lot of good if you had stayed inside the true Church?" He laughed jovially.

Captain Pepperell looked serious and answered by a Bible text. "'Come out from among them and be ye separate'; those were our sailing-orders," he said. "We could only be obedient to the heavenly vision."

"Well, at any rate," said Major Burwell genially, "I hope you of the Northern Colonies will not do in politics as you did in religion and break away from your moorings altogether. It may even be that the pirates will teach our Mother England that injustice kills trade, and that she is acting against her own interests in the Navigation Laws."

"It's a needed lesson but a costly one," answered Captain Pepperell, "and hard on those of us who go down to the sea in ships. The way to better things will be strewn with the wrecks of good vessels and the bones of good men for years to come.

When half an hour later they joined the ladies, they found Miss Cynthia at work upon her embroidery by the light of a blazing candelabrum, and Trix, looking pretty but miserable, sitting primly beside her, holding an embroidery-frame in her hand. She threw Tom an aggrieved glance as the boys entered the room, and jabbed her needle resentfully into her work. Her thread knotted, and she pricked her finger. Aunt Cynthia looked up from her green parrot, and unbuttoned her lips as though to speak, then sighed and closed them again with a hopeless snap. Evidently she despaired of her niece's progress in needle-work. Beatrix sucked her finger and frowned.

The two men talked about the Indians, and about Jamestown, and about Governor Berkeley's fine orchards across the river, until finally the Captain rose and, glancing out of the windows at the dark waters of the James and at the stern-light of the Nunquam Dormio, said, "I must be getting back to my ship. It's growing late, and I break anchor and go up-stream very early in the morning."

"If you must go," said the Major, "I'll have my man light you to the pier. Tom, call Sam, and tell him to bring a torch."

Archie and Tom both jumped to do this errand. They had been sitting in polite silence for a long time and were relieved to get a brief vacation from solemn talk. They groped their way quietly through the long corridor and paused at the door to see what was going on in the kitchen. By the dim light of a tallow candle they saw Mammy Jinny, enthroned among her pots and pans, holding a sable court. Becky, Pam, Jo, Enos, and Sam were all there, ready to wait upon the "white folks" when called, and Mammy was beguiling the time by a gruesome tale.

"It's jes like I'm tellin' you," they heard her say, "it war endurin' of the dark o' the moon, and I war gwine along from the big house to mah cabin. It war mighty late, fer Mars' George, he been gone all day, and it war plumb dark befo' he got home from Jamestown, and I had to git his supper. I war lopin' 'long home atterwards, and there wan't no grass growin' under my feet neither, when somethin' the very spit an' image of a man riz right up out'n de bushes by de buryin'-groun' and crope along by the fence, an' it made a moanin' sound like a squinch owl — Hoo-hoo-o-o it went," — here Mammy put her hands to her mouth and gave an unearthly sound which send the cold shivers down the backs of her hearers and made the whites of their eyes glisten like live coals in the shadowy room. "I ain't know no mo'," she went on, "fer I didn' tarry no longer. I jes lit out, an' I reckon they ain't no rabbit could 'a kotched me runnin'. I never teched ground mo'n three times between thar and mah cabin do'. Mah ol' man, he say it's some o' you low-down niggers playin' a trick on me, but I reckon I knows a ha'ant when I sees one! Yes, ma'am."

No one in the kitchen knew that the boys were in the corridor, and Tom saw a chance for mischief. Putting his hands to his mouth, he gave a faithful rendering of Mammy's low blood-curdling howl. The effect was magical. It was as if the kitchen had been loaded with a charge of negroes and had suddenly exploded. The door was flung open, and in an instant the room was empty of all but the two boys and  Mammy Jinny, and she was trying frantically to crawl under the kitchen table. Being too fat, she only succeeded in tipping it over and upsetting the candle. Tom sprang forward to rescue the candle and bumped into her in the dark.

"Oh, lawdy! lawdy! Mars' Debble, yo' sho'ly ain't gwine to put no conjure on me," screamed Mammy.

Tom shouted with laughter, and Mammy knew at once that it was only her bad boy playing a trick on her. It was not the first time Tom had teased her, and she let fly a random slap in the darkness. It landed where it should, and Tom interrupted his laughter with a surprised yelp.

"You obstreptious chile!" cried Mammy indignantly. "I ain't never brung you up since you was a runty li'l ol' baby to play tricks on yo' po' ol' Mammy. Go 'long now! You done skeert all dem niggers away, an' if you wants any of 'em you got to go git 'em yo'se'f fer I ain't gwine to he'p you. Not me!"

"Oh, come now, Mammy," coaxed Tom, and, still laughing, he stooped to light the candle again from a coal on the hearth.

"No, ma'am," growled Mammy, struggling to her feet. "Ain't gwine to do nuthin' for you no mo'! Yo' done skeer't me so I like to bus' myse'f wide open lopin' roun' yer in de dark."

"You scared your own self, Mammy," said Tom, "telling that wild tale about seeing things! You make up stories like that to scare the rest, and by and by you get to believe them yourself! You know very well you didn't see any such 'ha'ant.'"

"True as you live, Mars' Tom, I done so! I sho' did see it jus' like I done tol' 'em," Mammy insisted.

The frightened slaves, seeing the light and hearing the laughter, came creeping back into the kitchen, and soon the room rocked again with their mighty guffaws, as Mammy told how she had mistaken Tom for the devil in the dark and had upset the table. At last Tom remembered his errand, and Sam, at his order, kindled a fat pine knot and, holding it high above his head, led the way back through the dark corridor to the drawing-room. The Captain took his leave of Aunt Cynthia and Trix and, accompanied by the Major and the boys, followed Sam to the pier.

Out in the channel the lantern of the Nunquam Dormio made a dancing bridge of light from ship to shore. "Ship ahoy!" shouted the Captain, and "Aye, aye, sir" came promptly back from the anchor watch. Good-byes were said, and a moment later the Captain was in the small boat and was being rowed back to his ship.

The candles burned late at Honeywood that night, for after the Captain had gone, there were letters from England to be read. Archie's boxes had been carried to his room, which was just across a little hall from Tom's, and others belonging to the Major had been brought into the great hall and opened there. In them there were wonderful things.

There were silk gowns and scarlet sleeves and a Camlet cloak for Miss Cynthia, and velvet coats and ruffles of lace and finery of all sorts for the Major, and for Trix three pairs of satin shoes with silver buckles, and such an array of gay gowns that she felt like a princess in a fairy-tale and was almost reconciled to growing up and being a lady. She took the prettiest pair of slippers to bed with her and slept with them under her pillow that night.

IV. BAD NEWS

After the exciting events of the day the children slept soundly, and it was eight o'clock the next morning before Tom and Archie appeared. In the dining-room they found Aunt Cynthia in an impressive morning cap sitting behind the silver tea service, and Trix and the Major half through their breakfast.

"Well, my lad," said the Major to Archie when the boys had greeted Aunt Cynthia and Beatrix and were attacking their corn bread and bacon, "how do you find yourself this morning? Have you got your sea legs off yet?"

"The ground is still a little unsteady, sir," said Archie smiling, "but I'm right as a trivet and glad to be on hand and in such a pleasant place as Honeywood."

"That's a good word, my lad," said his uncle. "You'll need a day or two to see the place and begin to feel really at home here, so I've asked Mr. McNair to give you all a holiday. You'll have your lessons with him, of course, the same as Tom and Trix, but you needn't begin until you've had a chance to learn the ropes a bit."

Tom and Trix opened their mouths to cheer this announcement, but, remembering their manners just in time, said meekly, "Thank you, sir," instead, and were rewarded by a pleased smile from Aunt Cynthia, who was always at her best after she had had her morning cup of tea.

"I've been out to the stables already this morning," went on the Major, "and have selected a horse for you, Archie. Jo'll bring him around after breakfast; I haven't picked out a black boy to wait upon you yet, but I'll give you one as soon as I find one the right size, and meanwhile, Jo can do for both of you. He isn't overworked," and the Major chuckled.

"Oh, thank you, sir," cried Archie, his face beaming. "You are too good to me! I love riding and hated parting with my horse and dog when I left Kenmore."

"Every Virginian loves a good horse," said the Major.

"And every Englishman, too," said Archie.

"Yes," agreed the Major, "love of sports is in our blood. There's fine hunting and fishing about here. You'll not find life at Honeywood dull, I'm sure."

Just as they were finishing their breakfast, there was a clatter of hoofs outside, and all the children dashed outdoors, followed more slowly by the Major, to find Jo at the steps, holding the bridles of three spirited horses.

Tom vaulted at once into the saddle of his own gray mare, Lady, and Archie, after stroking the nose of Sintram, the black horse which was allotted to him, leaped to his back, while Jo held his hand for Trix to step upon in mounting her pretty brown Prince Charlie. Then they were off, and a brisk race to the tobacco-field proved beyond a doubt that all three were expert horsemen. The Major watched them, beaming with pride.

They were just entering the cart-path which led through the woods to the warehouse, when they were surprised to meet a man riding at a furious rate toward Honeywood. They drew their horses aside to let him pass, and then turned in their saddles to watch him as he sped past the tobacco-fields to the house.

"That's what they call the 'planter's pace' around here," said Tom to Archie. "I wonder what in the world he wants. Let's go back and see."

They turned their horses about and dashed up to the house just in time to hear the Major saying to the strange horseman: "Thank you. I'll go at once. I can get a mount across the river, I suppose. Don't let me detain you. You have a long way to go." And the man at once wheeled and dashed off toward the woods at the west.

"Oh, Father, what is it? Where are you going?" cried Trix, for she knew at once from his face that something was seriously wrong.

"Bad news," said the Major briefly. "That was a messenger from Curl's Wharf to tell me that the Indians have been making trouble over near York River. The Planters are going to give them a lesson they won't forget in a hurry. Where's Sam? Call Philpott. I must go at once!"

"Oh, Father!" cried Trix, turning white, "must you go?"

The Major was almost stern as he turned to his daughter. "Virginia has no use for cowards of either sex. Go and call your aunt."

Trix leaped from her horse, flung her bridle to Jo, and, without another word, ran on this errand. Tom and Archie had galloped off on the instant after Sam and the overseer, and in less than an hour from the time the messenger arrived at Honeywood, the Major, booted and spurred, was standing with Alexander McNair beside him in the stern of a large rowboat manned by six strong negro men, and was giving his final instructions to a group gathered on the pier to see him off.

Aunt Cynthia was there, looking pale but firm, with Beatrix and the boys beside her; and there also was Adam Philpott, his shifty eyes fixed on the Major's face. In the background hovered Mammy, fearfully clutching a package of cold turkey for 'Mars George,' which she had no chance to give him, and behind her a crowd of negroes, round-eyed and solemn, waited for his final orders.

"Philpott," said the Major, "I must leave the management of things here to you. I don't know just how long I shall be gone, but it is likely Captain Pepperell will be back to take on our cargo before I return. I have given you the keys to the warehouse, and you will take enough men from the field to help with the loading. Mr. McNair goes across the river with me to bring the boat back. Cynthia, I rely on you. Tom and Trix, — and Archie, too, — remember the motto of our house, '*Virtus omnia vincit*,' and, whatever happens, you will not fail for lack of courage, I know. The Indians have not yet appeared on this side of the river, and I'll guarantee we'll keep them so busy on the other side they won't have any time to plan any deviltry here, for a while anyway. Mammy, see that everybody gets enough to eat, and the rest of you mind the overseer and take good care of Miss Cynthia and the children until I get back."

"We will, Mars' George, we will," came back a chorus of rich negro voices. "Good-by! good-by! good-by!" and the boat shot out into the stream.

One by one the watchers on the pier melted away, until only the three children were left. They stayed, straining their eyes to catch a last glimpse of the gallant figure of the Major, until the boat became a mere speck on the broad surface of the river; then they went slowly back to the house and sat down on the porch steps in a row.

For a while no one said a word, for Tom and Trix could think of nothing but their father riding away into certain fighting and possible death, and Archie shared their anxiety. At last Tom gave himself a shake.

"It's no good just sitting around and moping," he said, "let's do something."

"I'll tell you what we'll do," said Trix; "we'll take the horses again and ride down to the warehouse."

"Anything is better than just waiting for things to happen," said Archie. "Let's make something happen!"

Fired by this idea, the three at once went to the stables, where Jo was rubbing down their horses, and in a few moments more they were galloping along the cart-path through the woods. There was no one at the warehouse when they reached it, but they dismounted and, tying their horses to trees a little distance away, began to show Archie about the place.

"Let's see if we can get inside," said Tom.

"You can't; you know you can't," said Trix. "You heard Father say old Pillbox had the keys."

Tom shook the door. It rattled loosely but did not give way. He shook it again, and then to their amazement there came from the inside of the building a low moaning owl cry, "Hoo-oo — oo-oo-oo."

The children gazed at each other in mute amazement and stood still to listen. They heard only the rustling of the leaves overhead and the thud of Lady's hoof as she impatiently pawed the ground and switched her tail to drive away the flies. There were no other sounds.

"Huh," said Tom finally, "we're as chicken-hearted as slaves. Nothing but an old owl up in the rafters! I'm not afraid. Let's peek through the cracks between the boards and show Archie the stuff Captain Pepperell is going to get when he comes back."

There were no windows in the building except an opening near the peak of the roof in the gable end, but there were yawning seams between the planks of which it was built. Still feeling a bit shaky, but laughing to hide their fears, they advanced upon the warehouse, and, led by Tom, climbed to the roof of a low "lean-to" and, crawling up the slope, applied their eyes to some wide cracks which they found there.

It took a few moments to become accustomed to the deep gloom within, but soon they could distinguish piles of lumber, and great casks filled with pitch or tobacco, or with stores of rum and molasses for the plantation.

"Look," said Tom to Archie. "You see that big hogshead over in the corner? The warehouse doors were left open one day last winter, and a bear got in and broke open that cask. It was full of rum then, and he lapped it up and got as drunk as a lord. He couldn't move! It's the skin of that bear that is now the rug beside your bed."

"What's that pile of dark stuff over in the corner?" asked Archie.

"Oh, more skins," said Tom carelessly. "Bear and beaver and deer-skins, and pelts of all kinds. The woods are full of game — wild horses too that have escaped, or colts that have grown up in the woods. Some day we'll see if we can't catch one. It's great sport."

They were just about to climb down again, when Trix suddenly seized Tom's arm and whispered, "Look, over in the corner — something's moving!"

They clutched each other, their hearts beating like trip-hammers, as they watched a queer shadow which seemed to crouch beside the heap of pelts and try to creep behind them.

For a moment they were too frightened to stir, then Archie recovered his presence of mind. "Oh, come on," he said, quite loudly, "I don't think it's interesting to look down that old hole. It's too dark to see anything anyway. Let's go back to the house." He turned away from the crack, and though his lips trembled so he could scarcely pucker them, he managed to whistle a tune as he led the way down the roof to the ground. Tom and Trix shot him an admiring glance and, taking their cue from him, strolled off toward the horses with every appearance of careless unconcern. If any one really was in the warehouse watching them, he would surely believe that they had seen nothing and had no suspicions.

Archie held his hand for Trix to mount, while Tom unhitched Prince Charlie, and when she was safely in the saddle, the two boys leaped upon their horses and all three dashed off through the woods in the direction of Honeywood as if all the bears in the forest were after them.

Adam Philpott reined up his big black horse as they passed the tobacco-field and hailed them. "Where are you going so fast?" he called out with a laugh. "You look as if you had seen a ghost. Or is it a race? I bet my money on the gray mare if it is."

Tom opened his mouth to tell the overseer what they had seen, but Trix cut him short.

"It is a race," she said excitedly, "and I'm going to win it myself," and away she dashed, crying out, "Catch me if you can," over her shoulder to Archie and her brother, and instantly they were all off again at the "planter's pace," never slacking speed until their steaming mounts reached the stable.

They held a brief conference as they walked to the house.

"Don't say a word to the overseer or Aunt Cynthia, or any one, about this yet," said Trix.

"But," objected Tom, "Father said old Pillbox was in charge, and if there's any mischief brewing in the warehouse he ought to know it."

"Maybe it was just one of the negroes we saw trying to steal some rum," said Archie.

Tom stopped suddenly, struck by the memory of Mammy Jinny's story in the kitchen the night before.

"Maybe Mammy really did see something after all," he said. "This thing crept along just the way she said the 'ha'ant' did, and, by Jupiter, that was just the same noise she said it made! That was no owl we heard!"

"You don't really believe in ghosts!" said Archie.

"No-o — not exactly — of course not," said Tom, doubtfully. "All the same, queer things do happen that you can't account for. You can't make the negroes think there aren't any! They'll all tell you they have seen 'em."

As they passed the kitchen, Mammy Jinny came out to ring the great plantation bell to call them to dinner. She paused with her hand on the rope as she saw the children, and it was plain that her spirits were low.

"Ain't no use cookin' nuthin'," she grumbled. "Ain't nobody want to eat nuthin'. Miss Cynthy she stay up in her room. She say she got a headache. Mr. McNair ain't got back yet. I got a risin' in my haid myse'f. Ain't nuthin' gwine right on this here plantation, nohow."

"Why, what's the matter now, Mammy?" said Beatrix. "There hasn't anything new happened, has there?"

"Nuthin' new ain't happened yit," said Mammy darkly, "but I lay it's gwine ter. Las' night they was a black cat yowled at my do', and everybody knows that black cats is the Old Boy hisself! Nuthin' ain't gwine right on this yer place sence I seed that ha'ant."

For all her low spirits, Mammy had cooked a wonderful dinner of fried chicken and hominy, and in spite of their worries the children ate it and felt much better. Just as they were leaving the table Alexander McNair returned with the boat, and they dashed down to the dock to meet him.

He reported that the Major had joined a company of planters gathered on the other side of the river, and that they were riding away under the leadership of young Nathaniel Bacon to the York River to punish the Indians. There were terrible tales of murders on the far side of the York Peninsula, but the Major had told him to carry word to Miss Cynthia that there was no cause for fear as yet, for the scene of these horrors was still far away from Honeywood.

V. THE TREE HOUSE

From the dock the children wandered on down the river-bank in the direction of the Big Oak. It was a lovely May afternoon, warm and bright, and the air was full of cheerful sounds. Redbirds whistled in the cedars, and a mockingbird, hidden in the box hedge, poured forth a medley of liquid notes. A flock of geese waddled solemnly down the bank and sailed away up the river like a little fleet, poking their bills into the mud along the water's edge in search of dainties suited to their taste. From the distant tobacco-fields came now and then faint snatches of song and laughter, as the negroes bent to their tasks. Everything was so peaceful and quiet that the fears of the morning no longer seemed real to the children.

"I just wonder," said Archie, "if we really did see anything moving in the warehouse after all. How could anything get in if the door was locked?"

"There might be a loose board somewhere," said Tom, "but what I can't explain is that wailing noise — just exactly like Mammy Jinny's."

Archie laughed. "Well, Mammy Jinny's was like an owl's," he said. "The warehouse is dark enough to just suit an owl. It's a joke on us if we were scared at nothing at all. Let's go down there again tomorrow morning."

"Let's go up in the tree house, now," said Beatrix. "I always feel safe up there, and you haven't seen it yet, Archie."

"What's the tree house?" said Archie.

"You'll see," answered Tom, "only you must promise you'll never, never tell any one. It's a secret. Nobody knows a thing about it but just Trix and me."

"I promise," said Archie.

Following their usual custom of approaching the Big Oak by a round-about way, Tom led them back from the river through a corn-patch and past the overgrown little graveyard. Then they circled back through the long grass toward the river, crossed the neck of the little peninsula, and stood under the wide-spreading branches of the oak.

"Hitchity hatchet, my little red jacket, and up I go," said Tom, swinging himself into the tree, and Archie, agile as a monkey, sprang after him. Trix followed, and in a minute more Archie was being shown the shields and spears and their treasure-house in the hollow limb.

"Crickey!" said Archie enthusiastically — or if it wasn't "crickey" it was something else. "What a jolly old place! We can have no end of fun up here!"

"We must make some more spears and shields and things," said Tom, "and then we can play tournament under the tree, and everything."

"Oh, Tom!" cried Trix, "won't it be nice to have two knights? You see," she explained to Archie, "when there was only Tom and me, I always had to be the other knight and all the ladies."

"That's too much for any girl," laughed Archie, taking the books which Trix handed him and seating himself on the floor to look at them. "Hi!" he cried, opening "The Tempest." "Why, I saw this played in London."

"Did you truly," gasped the Twins. They had never seen even the outside of a theater in their lives. "Oh, Archie, tell us all about it."

They seated themselves on the floor beside him, and there followed an enchanted hour while Archie read the play aloud, telling about the stage and the actors and the costumes as he went along, until it almost seemed to Tom and Trix as if they could see it being played before their very eyes. Archie had a quick ear for music, and when he came to Ariel's song, sang it softly, as he had heard it sung in the theater —

"Come unto these yellow sands,
  And then take hands.
Curtsied when you have, and kiss'd
  The wild waves whist" —

He had got as far as the final chorus of "Hark, hark! Bow-wow. The watch-dogs bark!" when they were jolted out of their make-believe world by the distant barking of a real dog.

"That's Duke," said Tom. "He only barks like that when something's wrong. I wonder what ails him!"

He climbed down to a lower limb, and peered through the branches toward the corn-field.

Archie and Trix stretched themselves flat on the floor of the tree house and looked, too. In a moment they saw the burly figure of Adam Philpott come out of the bushes which hid the burying-ground. He had a stick in his hand, and though he was quite far away, they caught the distant echo of an oath as he threw the stick at Duke. There was a surprised yelp, as the stick struck, and then Duke turned tail and ran as fast as he could on three legs to the house, yelping all the way.

"The old brute!" muttered Tom. "I wish Duke had bitten him."

The overseer looked cautiously about and slunk back out of sight in the bushes, as if he feared some one might have been with the dog. In a few moments he appeared again and turned in the direction of the river, following much the same path the children had taken an hour before. Tom scrambled back into the tree house, and stretched himself beside his sister and his cousin.

"What in the world makes him act like that? Do you suppose he's coming here?" breathed Trix.

Tom shook his head, and the tree house became as still as the graveyard itself.

"He's got a gun on his shoulder. I reckon he's just going down to the river to shoot some wild ducks," whispered Tom. "He isn't coming here, that's sure. Maybe Mammy Jinny asked him to get some game for to-morrow's dinner."

The man had now reached the edge of the cypress forest which bordered the river to the eastward, and was soon hidden from their sight. They were beginning to breathe easily again, when from farther down the river they heard the low owl cry followed by the soft dip of paddles in the water, and around a little bend came a canoe with a man in it. It was too far away to see very clearly, but they could tell that his skin was dark.

The man in the boat was paddling very slowly and looking along the wooded shore as if he expected some one. Soon the watchers saw the overseer step from out the undergrowth and get into the canoe, which was immediately driven swiftly forward directly toward the Big Oak.

The children could hardly breathe for excitement. They hung over the edge of the tree house in a row, and not one of them moved a hair as the canoe slipped with a soft swishing sound among the tall reeds of the marsh — almost underneath their hiding-place. They could see the tops of the two heads and the tip of the overseer's gun, and they could hear quite plainly everything the men said though they spoke in low tones.

"This is the safest spot on the plantation," said the overseer's voice. "There's not a soul about here to see us, and if there were, the reeds would hide us. Now tell me what happened? Something did, I know, for those meddlesome brats were down at the warehouse this morning, and when they came back there were white as paper." (There was a wrathful wiggle in the tree house. Meddlesome brats, indeed!) "Did they see you?"

"No, Massa, they ain't never see me," said the other voice. "I thought it was you rattling the door, so I give the call — but I never did open it. They ain't never know nuthin' about me, for a I hear one of 'em say, 'It ain't no use lookin' in there; can't see nuthin' anyway,' — and then they went off whistlin' a tune and got on they hosses and rid away. I spied 'em through a crack."

"You should have kept your mouth shut, you fool Mustee, till you knew it was me and nobody else," said the overseer angrily. "Another such blunder and I'll break every bone in your body."

At the word "Mustee," Trix could not help a shudder. Mustees were half-breeds, of Indian and negro parentage, and they were said to have all the faults of both races. Every one feared them.

The smothered voice of the overseer went on: "Listen to what I tell you now, and keep your wits about you. Everything is fixed for us, and the job must be done to-night. The master's away, and won't be back for two or three days anyway. Nobody home but an old lady" (how Aunt Cynthia would have resented that!), "three children, and an old owl of a near-sighted Scotchman, and some niggers. That's all. Where is your ship?"

"Round yander — in a backwater where it can't be seen from the river," answered the Mustee.

"Well, get back to it as soon as you can, and tell the Captain to be at the warehouse dock at three o'clock in the morning. I'll sleep there with the keys. We'll have the whole load aboard and be off down the river before any one is up on the plantation, and that'll be the end of this dog's life for me. Mind — there's a whole barrel of rum with the rest of the stuff."

"I'll mind that, Massa," chuckled the Mustee, smacking his lips. "You can trus' the Captain. He won't miss a chance like that. Heh-heh — this job is too easy — it's like stealin' from a baby!"

"You keep your tongue in your head and don't take any chances," warned the overseer. "When you come to the warehouse, you'll have to give the signal, and you give it three times so there'll be no mistake; and now I've got to get a couple of ducks for dinner to-morrow. Nobody ever comes down this way, and you can take me round to the marsh by the warehouse safely enough. It's alive with ducks round there!"

The canoe slid out from its hiding-place among the reeds, and, speeded by the current, went swiftly down the river, keeping close to shore.

When the canoe had passed out of sight round the bend in the river, the three children looked at each other with white, terror-stricken faces. Trix was the first to find her voice.

"Pirates! — right here at Honeywood!" she shuddered. "Oh, did

you see that Mustee's face? Little mean eyes and great thick lips" — she covered her face with her hands as if to shut out the horrible memory — "just like Caliban! Oh, why did I ever say I wanted adventures to happen?"

"You got your wish," said Tom grimly. "Things are happening fast enough."

"The question is what to do," said Archie practically. "You remember what your father said about our motto."

"Yes," groaned Tom, "and if '*virtus*' is every going to help us, now it's chance!"

"Courage isn't going to do a thing unless somebody's got it, and there's nobody but us to have it," said Archie soberly. "Father used to say, 'Without danger there's no such thing as courage.'"

"There's danger enough for any amount of it this time," said Tom, "but we can't stop to think about danger. We've just got to think about how we can save the goods at the warehouse. It's the entire product of the plantation for the winter, and if the pirates get it, I don't know what Father will do. He had to sell his tobacco at such a low price last fall on account of having to send it England and nowhere else that I know he is hard pressed for money, and he just must not lose the winter's work too."

For a while the three sat still, thinking as they had never thought before. Finally Trix lifted her head, which had been buried in her hands. "I've thought of something," she said.

"So have I," said Tom, "but you tell yours."

"First," said Trix, "we've got to get help. We haven't any one here to count on but ourselves and Sandy, and Aunt Cynthia and Mammy."

"What good would Aunt Cynthia and Mammy be?" said Tom scornfully. "Aunt Cynthia would die of fright at the butt end of a gun. She couldn't shoot one to save her life, and as for Mammy — you're crazy!"

"I'm not," said Trix fiercely, "wait and you'll see! Mammy is afraid of ghosts and things like that, but she would lay down her life for us, and Aunt Cynthia isn't a coward if she is a lady."

Tom interrupted. "Even if every one of us — Mammy and all — were regular heroes, we'd have to get help," he said, "and there is only one way to get it that I can see. We've got to find Captain Pepperell."

"I've thought of that, too," said Archie, "but how? We can't row very far up the river ourselves and back in time. We've only got until three o'clock in the morning to do this job, and it must be three in the afternoon now! And nobody knows how far up-stream the Captain may be."

"It's a long way through the woods just to Brandon, and Westover is ever so far beyond that and on the other side of the river besides," said Tom. "The planters will have gone to fight the Indians, and we can't get help from them."

"Can't you use the slaves?" asked Archie.

"They aren't allowed any fire-arms," said Tom. "They're faithful, but most of 'em would be rabbits in a case like this. No, nothing to depend on there."

Archie rose. "Only twelve hours to turn the trick," said he. "Let's find Captain Pepperell as quick as we can. He's the bravest man on earth and used to pirates! You ought to have seen him when they chased us coming over! He'll know just what to do."

Trix took the precious books and hid them carefully in the hollow limb, and the three children climbed quickly down from the tree. They were starting on the run for the house when Tom stopped them.

"Here, hold your horses!" said he. "We don't save any time by running before we decide how we are going to get to the Captain."

"There's only one way," said Trix decidedly. "We'll have to go on horseback up the trails and keep looking up the river until we see the Nunquam Dormio. When we see her, we'll have to find some way of reaching her and speaking to the Captain, but we can't decide that now."

"All right," said Tom. "Now let's hurry."

But Trix had thought of a new difficulty.

"We mustn't let Aunt Cynthia know where we have gone or she'll be worried to death, and we've got to get off before the overseer gets back. He'd certainly suspect something if he saw us ride off through the woods at this hour — especially if we didn't get back for supper." She clapped her hands distractedly to her head. "I have it," she said. "Mammy Jinny! She'll help us out. We'll ask her for some bacon and other stuff to eat and tell her we're going a little way up the river to cook our supper and may not be back until dark. If Aunt Cynthia's head still aches, she won't know anything about it until supper time, anyway."

Archie looked admiringly at Trix. "You certainly have your wits about you," he said, "but it seems to me Tom and I should do this alone. It isn't a job for a girl."

"Oh," said Tom, "you don't know Trix. It's no good to tell her that. She'll go if any one does, and you can't stop her."

Trix did not even notice the suggestion. She was already speeding toward the house, and in a very short time the three presented themselves at the kitchen door. Mammy was sitting on the threshold paring potatoes. She listened to their plea for food with disapproval.

"How come yo' all gone plumb crazy?" she asked pointedly. "Miss Trix can't cook nuthin' fit to eat, an' I was fixin' fer to give yo' a surprise fer your supper, an' I ain't goin' to tell yo' all what 'tis, nuther."

"Oh, Mammy," coaxed Trix, "just this once. We'll be back by dark, and you can feed us some more then, if we're hungry."

Mammy shook her head violently. "I dunno what Miss Cynthy'll say," she grumbled, "but she give out not to discommotion her, an' I suttinly ain't gwine to break her res' for no sich foolishness," and, rising, she waddled away to the pantry.

By the time Solly had the horses saddled she had the basket of food ready for them. Tom hung it from his saddle-horn, and the three rode off, waving their hands gaily to Mammy Jinny in the kitchen door. As they entered the dark forest trail to the westward they heard the distinct crack of a gun in the direction of the warehouse.

"There's old Pirate Pillbox after his ducks," said Tom. "We are off without his knowing it, anyway."

Once safely screened by the trees, they urged their horses forward at full speed.

"We'll have to make all the time we can now," said Tom, "for it will be so dark coming back we can't see the trail at all."

For a while they rode swiftly on without a word. Then Tom said: "The trail runs pretty near the water here. I'll get off and take a look up the river to see if the boat is in sight."

He threw his bridle-rein to Archie and crashed through the underbrush to the shore. In a few moments he returned. "Nothing in sight," he reported, and, vaulting into the saddle again, he led the way up the trail.

For an hour they kept on their way, stopping now and then to scan the broad expanse of the James. Then at last the trees began to thin out a little. There were glimpses of an opening beyond, and in a few moments more they were in the open field of Brandon plantation. The stately house overlooking the river showed no sign of life as they approached it, but beyond many slaves were at work in the tobacco-fields. They dismounted here and, passing through the garden to the river-front again, sought the Nunquam Dormio. It was nowhere in sight.

"The river makes a bend here, and we may get beyond her without knowing it," said Tom, "but we'll cut cross the point. From there we can look over to Weyanoke, and if she isn't there, she is probably at Westover, and that's too far up. We never could make it in time!"

They rode on as fast as they could, and in another half-hour reached a place on the bend of the river from which they could look up-stream for some distance. They were overjoyed to see the ship lying at the end of a long dock across the river.

"Oh," cried Trix, "there she is, bless her heart, with her nose pointing up-stream. That means she's not been to Westover yet. If we can only catch her before she leaves Weyanoke!"

"Yes, but, —" said Tom, "how are we going to get to her? We haven't wings, and there's no magic here to help us out, as there was on Prospero's island!"

Again they were plunged into despair.

"We'll have to ride back to Brandon and get a boat from there somehow," said Tom. "It's a long way to go, but it's our only chance. Come on!"

He wheeled his horse and was plunging back into the forest, when Trix gave a smothered cry.

"There's a canoe," she said.

There, indeed, was a canoe, just coming into sight from behind the boughs of a fallen tree at the river's edge. In it was an Indian!

The children instantly rode into the underbrush, but the horses made such a crashing noise they realized at once that hiding was out of the question.

"We've just got to chance it," said Tom. "Anyway, if he were on the war-path he wouldn't be here," and he boldly rode Lady to the water's edge and hailed the canoe.

The Indian gazed at them stolidly without any sign of understanding as Tom made urgent signals to him to come to the shore.

"It's the only hope," said Tom over his shoulder. "I'm going to get him to take me over to the ship if I can, but we'll have to give him something." He groped in the basket and held up the bacon, then held out the basket toward the Indian.

"Oh, Tom," said Trix in an agonized undertone, "suppose he's unfriendly! Suppose he takes you somewhere else! Suppose he gets you out in the river —" She could not finish the sentence.

"It's the only way," Tom answered doggedly. Again he beckoned the Indian and pointed to the basket and to the ship and made signs that he wished to be taken across the river. Meanwhile Archie had been doing some quick thinking. He now leaped to the ground, tossing his bridle rein to Trix, and ran to the bank.

"If any one goes, I'm going," he said firmly. "You see for yourself, Tom, one of us must stay with Trix. You know the way back and I don't. I know the Captain and the sailors and the ship and you don't," and, without waiting for a reply, he reached down and, tearing the silver buckles from his shoes, held them up in one hand and the basket in the other for the Indian to see.

Apparently the combined inducements of the basket and the buckles worked powerfully on the Indian's intelligence. He pointed to the ship, to the canoe, to the basket and buckles, and back again to the ship, and a grin of understanding broke over his face. He brought the canoe to shore. Archie tossed him his price and sprang into the canoe, fortunately without tipping it over. The Indian grunted and at once turned his light craft toward the farther shore.

"Sit very still," called Tom, "and get the Captain to come back to Brandon at once. We'll meet you there."

"If he can do it he will, I know. Watch until you see the sails go up, and then hurry back to the dock," called Archie.

For what seemed an endless time the brother and sister stood on the shore, anxiously watching the tiny boat as it breasted the waves of the river. They breathed a great sign of relief as it reached the dock on the farther side and disappeared from view.

"That's one danger past," said Tom. "He got there all right, anyway."

They strained their eyes to see any signs of life on the ship, but it was too far away.

"Oh, what can have happened?" said Trix, almost tearfully, beating her hands together as the long minutes passed. "It seems as if everybody must be asleep or dead on that boat."

"There's nothing to do but wait," Tom answered, "and be plucky." Then he added, "Remember about *Virtus*."

Trix stiffened in her saddle at this challenge to her courage, and just then — oh, joy! — they saw a white sail on the Nunquam Dormio rising slowly above the hull!

"She's coming! she's coming!" cried Trix, and, leading Archie's horse by the bridle-rein, the two dashed back into the deepening shadows of the trail.

VI. THE PLOT THICKENS

During the ride back to Brandon, Beatrix looked over her shoulder more than once, for their way led through a dense forest. The sun was already sinking lower and lower in the west, the shadows were deepening on the trail, and it would soon be time for wild beasts to be prowling. Moreover, how in the world would they be able to account for such an absence from home? What would Aunt Cynthia say? Beatrix wished her aunt no harm, but she fervently hoped that her headache would continue until they reached Honeywood again.

With such thoughts as these pounding through their heads they galloped along, keeping a sharp lookout to the right and left for new dangers. As they neared the clearings of Brandon, Tom drew rein and, waiting until Trix was beside him, said in a low tone: "I think we'd better stop this side of the dock, where we can't be seen from the house. We might be mistaken for Indians or prowlers, and get into a lot of trouble. Explanations would take time, and we can watch for the boat easily enough anywhere along the shore."

They turned aside from the trail and, tethering the horses among the trees, sat down on a log at the water's edge to wait. The sun was now almost down to the tops of the western trees and the whip-poor-wills were already piercing the evening shadows with their lonely cry. They sat there with the night sounds pulsing all about them, and with their own hearts beating so loudly they could hear them, and still no ship. Things began to look very serious. Every moment's delay was a threat to their plans, and they were still a long way from home.

Then there was a crackling sound along the river-bank just beyond them, and a dark figure came toward them out of the shadows. For an instant their hearts stopped beating and stood still. Then Archie's voice came softly out of the gloom, and they began again.

"Tom! Trix!" he called.

"Archie!" they exclaimed. "How in the world did the boat get by us? We've been here watching every minute."

"Simple enough," answered Archie. "It didn't."

"Then how did you get here?" gasped Trix.

"The Captain sent me ashore above here in the small boat. He thought he'd better keep the ship out of sight of Brandon. The slaves come in from the fields at sundown, and somebody might see us, spread the alarm, and spoil the plot. He'll bring the ship down after dark. I knew I'd find you at the dock if not before."

"All right," said Tom, "we needn't stop for your story now. We'll get the horses and make use of every minute of daylight for getting through the woods."

Without another word they ran to their mounts and were soon flying along across the open stretches of Brandon toward the Honeywood trail. There followed an hour of hard riding, but, fortunately for them, the moon rose early that night, and patches of moonlight here and there through the trees grayed the darkness enough so they could follow the trail, and at last they reached the home acres and came in sight of the big house. Candles were glimmering from the kitchen, but the big house was dark except for a light in the hall. They drew their three horses together and held a council of war.

"We've got to tell the same story when we get in," said Archie. "I daren't stop now to tell you the plan. It will keep until after we eat, for our next move doesn't begin until everybody else is abed."

"They'll have the whole place roused to hunt for us if we don't show up now," agreed Tom, "and this is no safe place to talk, anyway," so, though he and Trix were both nearly bursting with curiosity to hear what Archie had to say, they threw their bridle-reins to a boy who was waiting at the stable door, and started on foot for the house.

On the way they met Alexander McNair, his hair blowing wildly about his head and his face haggard with anxiety. He held up his hand to stop them. "Where have you been, you little deils," he began. "If your guid aunt were not sick wi' a headache, 'tis likely she would be dead of fright! I'm laith to scaud ye, but ye've no call to go rampagin' through the woods at this time o' night with Indians abroad and all."

"Dear Mr. McNair," wheedled Beatrix, taking his hand and smiling beguiling up at him, "you mustn't scold us! We did have a call to go, truly! It's very important you should trust us this once, and as soon as we possibly can we'll tell you all about it. Right after we've had something to eat!"

"Yes, please, Mr. McNair," begged the boys, "just as soon as we can we'll meet you in the school-room."

"And, oh, Mr. McNair, won't you *please* pretend you knew all about it and weren't worried — especially before the overseer if he's about?" added Trix.

Mr. McNair gave a shrewd glance at their pale faces, had the wisdom to conclude that there must be some good reason for their strange behavior, and wisely nodded his head. As they reached the kitchen door he even played their game by saying in a loud voice: "Ye'll come to the school-room in half an hour. I want to look over to-morrow's work with you."

"All right!" answered the children, and burst in at the kitchen door.

"Whar yo' been?" demanded Mammy, confronting them with an accusing face. "I couldn't go to ma cabin nohow, without I knowed you was safe."

"We went quite a long way up the river, Mammy," said Trix, "and we lost our basket."

"Lawsee, honey, ain't yo' all had no supper yit?" said Mammy, in horror-stricken tones. "I lay yo' is nigh starvation," and, rising, she began at once to get them something to eat.

"I tell you what you do, Mammy," said Trix; "you put some cold things on a tray and bring it over to the school-house! Mr. McNair wants to see us about some lessons, and he doesn't like to wait."

"I sho'ly will, my pore li'l lamb," said Mammy, and the three drifted quietly out of the kitchen.

Tom and Archie went at once to the school-house, while Trix tiptoed up the stairs to her aunt's room.

"Aren't you feeling any better, Aunty?" she asked, through the door. A gentle snore was her only answer, and, greatly relieved, she slipped quietly down again and joined the conspirators in the school-room.

She found Archie and Tom seated one on each side of Mr. McNair whispering into his ears, while that poor gentleman turned his astonished face from one to the other as if his head were on a swivel as he listened.

"Come on, Trix," said Archie, rising to give her a chair. "We've told as far as getting back here, and now my story begins. Here's the outline of Captain

Pepperell's plan. He's sailing down the river now, without any lights on, and the boat is going to drop anchor just above Honeywood. Then about eleven o'clock, when every one is in bed and asleep, we slip out of the house and go down to the river. We signal to the Captain; it's moonlight and he can see us. And then the Captain comes ashore. He'll bring with him some trustworthy men who've sailed the seven seas and know pirates from *A* to *izzard*, he says, and then he'll tell us what to do next. All we've got to do is to do what he says."

Just then Mammy appeared at the door with a tray laden with cold ham, bread and butter, cake, and other good things to eat. Hearing a step outside, Sandy McNair said in a loud tone to Archie, "And how far-r have you read in Cæsar-r, my lad?"

"Two books," answered Archie promptly, and no one, not even the overseer himself could have guessed from their bland faces that they had been talking about anything but Latin lessons all the time.

Mammy set down the tray but lingered. Evidently something was on her mind.

"What is it, Mammy?" said Tom.

"It's this yere ha'ant, Mars' Tom," said poor Mammy. "I'm jes studyin' 'bout gittin' back to mah cabin. I ain't afeard o' nuthin' by daylight, but I don't hanker atter no traffic with ghosts atter sundown."

"I'll gang a piece wi' ye, Mammy," said Sandy. "The youngsters can eat and look over their lessons while I'm gone."

"I ain't never seen it but once," said Mammy, "but that time nigh give me appleplexy. It sho'ly is might kin' of yo', Mars McNair, and I ain't gwine ter fergit it."

She went out the door followed by the tutor, and the three children were left alone in the school-room.

"Isn't Sandy an old dear?" said Trix as the door closed behind him.

"I thought old Sandy hadn't a drop of blood in him but was just stuffed with parts of speech and things like that," said Tom. "Why, he's got as much juice in him as anybody has, even if he does know a lot!"

They were jut finishing their lunch, when Mr. McNair came in with a very wide-awake look on his face, and closed the door carefully behind him before he spoke.

"'Tis as weel I went wi' her," he said, "for she boxed the compass wi' her eyes all the way hame. Just as we were almost at her door she was glowerin' round, and what did she do but catch sight of a dar-rk figure moving along the car-rt path toward the warehouse! Of course, I kenned it was Philpott, but she took it for the ghost and let a screech that would have shamed an Indian, bolted inside her cabin, and slammed the door behind her. I screamed to her through the door that I would put a mark on it that would keep the ghosts and bogles all away, and now she thinks I'm a regular old Prospero." Mr. McNair chuckled. "I thought it a canny thing to keep an eye on that auld villain's whereabouts, and now we ken weel he's gone to the warehouse, as he said he would."

"Oh, good for you, Sandy!" cried Tom, quite forgetting in his excitement to use Mr. McNair's proper name. Trix looked at Tom in horror, and he stopped, abashed, and clapped his hand over his unlucky mouth.

Sandy's eyes twinkled. "That's nane so bad a name, laddie," he said kindly. "Mr. McNair it is in the school-room, to be sure, but fighting pir-r-rates is a different thing altogether, and 'Sandy' will do verra weel then. It takes less time to say it in a pinch."

Tom grinned cheerfully at Sandy, and from that moment the children and he were no longer pupils and teacher, but equal partners in a dangerous enterprise.

"We ought to put the lights out for a while, so no one will suspect there's anything unusual going on," said Tom. "Old Pirate Pillbox may have spies about for all we know."

"Verra true, verra true," said Sandy. "You lads maun tak' a little rest, and you Beatrix, maun stay in your room. Tonight's wor-rk is no job for a lady."

"Oh, Sandy," implored Trix, "I'm not a lady yet, and I should simply die to be left here by myself and not know what you were all doing! Haven't I been just as good as you so far?" she demanded, turning to the boys.

"You're the pluckiest girl I ever say," said Archie, and Tom added: "Oh, let her come, Sandy. You might as well — she will, anyway!"

Sandy shook his head. "Ye'll take your own r-r-responsibility then," he said, his "r's" rumbling fearsomely. "I wash my hands of it," and Trix took this for consent.

"You go to your-r r-rooms now," urged Sandy. "I'll keep watch and wake you before the first cock-cr-row."

He lit three candles from his own and gave one to Trix. The two boys escorted her to the big house and stood at the foot of the stairs until she reached her room, then Tom made a tour of the doors to see that they were fastened, before he and Archie went to their own quarters over the school-room. In a short time every light on the plantation was out, and the whole place appeared wrapped in slumber.

Trix was too excited to think of lying down, so she sat by her window and listened to the whip-poor-wills and tree-toads. An owl hooted, and she jumped as if a gun had gone off, thinking for an instant it might be a signal from the Mustee. One window in her room overlooked the river; the other was directly opposite Tom's room in the school-house. All of the windows were open, and she could hear faint sounds as the boys moved restlessly about in the darkness of their rooms across the way. After waiting for what seemed an endless time, she heard her name spoken in a low tone and, springing to her eastern window, saw by the light of the moon that Archie and Tom were signaling to her.

"Sandy says it's time to go," they whispered. Trix nodded and waved her hand to them, then, opening her door, started stealthily down the stairs.

If Aunt Cynthia should wake! Or if Becky, who slept on a rug at Aunt Cynthia's door should hear her! She crept from stair to creaking stair in her stocking-feet, and finally reached the hall door, which gave such an alarming squeak as she opened it that for a moment her heart would have been in her boots if her boots had not at that very moment been in her hands!

On the porch she found Sandy and the boys waiting for her. She put on her shoes sitting on the bottom step, and then the four slipped quietly into the shadow of the box hedge which framed the garden, and made their way in silence to the river's edge.

It was now midnight, and light clouds were scudding before the face of the moon, which was fast dipping toward the west. The four conspirators reached the riverbank and eagerly scanned the silvery surface of the water. Out in midstream they were soon able to discern the shadowy outlines of the Nunquam Dormio.

"She looks sound asleep enough now, in spite of her name," Tom whispered to Archie.

"She'll wake up, never fear," Archie answered.

Soon they heard the soft splash of oars, and a small boat loomed out of the shadows and ground its keel on the shore, and out of it stepped Captain Pepperell, followed by six stalwart sailors armed with pistols and knives.

"Here," said the Captain to Sandy, "are six men who have sailed the seven seas and met pirates in most of them, and they hate pirates as they do sharks. You can trust them perfectly. My advice is that you let this man," laying his hand on the shoulder of a young giant who stood beside him, "lead the land forces. He's a fighting Irishman named Kennedy. I'll take charge of the attack by water myself."

Then he caught sight of Beatrix. "What on earth are you doing here?" he exclaimed. "This is no place for a girl!"

"It's too late, Captain, she's her-r-e," said Sandy, "and her-r-e she's bound to be. She'll not get in the way. The lass has as good a head as any lad and more pluck than most."

Trix kept silent. "Then she'll go on the ship," said the Captain shortly. "She'll be safer there than on land, anyway. Now listen, all of you. I've had the whole story from Archie here, so there's no need of going over that. These men know it too. Here's the plan. You, Kennedy, will take these men and Mr. McNair and go down the trail to the warehouse as quietly as you can. When you get there, creep up to the door and give the signal he arranged with the Mustee. That signal must be given just right or the whole plot may fail. You, Tom, would better do that. Are you sure you remember, Tom? How does it go?"

Tom gave a low owl cry.

"That's all right," said the Captain. "Mind you do it at the right time, Tom and you, Archie, go on the boat with me. You aren't needed ashore, and you might be useful afloat." He turned again to the men. "If things go right, Philpott will open the warehouse door when he hears the signal. Kennedy will be ready to grab him, and these two men will rope him at once. They've got the ropes. Then you must tie him up and gag him, so he can't give any warning. When the real Mustee comes along, all will be quiet and you'll be there to welcome him. Meanwhile, I'll keep at lookout until I see the pirate ship tie up to the dock and the men go ashore. You will have settled the Mustee by that time. I'll creep up into range, and if I don't miss my guess, we can separate the men from the ship — and the rest is easy. The Nunquam Dormio carries four guns. I'll train them on their ship, and if there's any one left on board I don't believe he'll stay long! But if you value your lives, don't go near the end of the dock. I shall direct my fire lengthwise of the ship's deck, but in the scrimmage a shot might go astray. Now wait until I get back to the ship, and then you start."

"Aye, aye, sir," said the sailors, and "Aye, aye, sir," said Trix and the boys.

There was one man waiting to row the Captain back, and Trix and Archie followed him obediently into the boat, which melted at once into the shadows of the night.

Soon over the waters came the Captain's voice calling softly to the mate from the small boat, "Ship ahoy."

"Aye, aye, sir."

"Man the windlass, heave short, and get ready to break out the anchor, then take us aboard."

"Aye, aye, sir."

In a moment gray shadows manned the windless brakes, and a sailor's chanty floated out over the water.

"We're homeward bound, I hear them say,
  Good-by, fare you well,
  Good-by, fare you well —"

They got no farther, for the Captain's angry voice called from the small boat, "Belay that noise there," and sudden silence fell upon the waters, broken only by the creaking of windlass.

The watchers on shore waited until they could see the shadowy ship, its anchor having been lifted, begin to move slowly downstream, then they started under Tom's guidance on their stealthy journey toward the warehouse.

"We'd best keep as far as possible from the Honeywood buildings," said Tom, "for we don't want to wake either the dogs or the negroes," and he led them by a round-about path back of the stables and the tobacco-fields to the trail at the point where it entered the woods.

"Now," he murmured, "lift your feet high and step softly, so you won't stumble over any roots."

Silently the eight figures moved slowly through the thick darkness of the woods, and after a long march at last reached the little clearing where the warehouse stood. Silently they scanned the dark river. There was as yet no sight of the pirate ship. Silently the two men with the ropes crept forward and placed themselves on one side of the door, and silently Kennedy took his station on the other. Sandy and Tom were close beside Kennedy with the other men behind them.

"Now," whispered Kennedy in Tom's ear, and he instantly gave the owl call, which was made all the more owl-like by the trembling of his voice.

"Hoo-oo-oo-oo-oo-oo-oo-oo-oo-oo," he wailed.

With their hearts knocking against their ribs they waited. Then there was a shuffling sound within, the door swung outward, and in the opening appeared the face of the overseer. When he saw the group of men outside instead of the one man he expected, his right hand instantly flew to his belt and swung upward carrying a knife, while with his left he made a futile effort to seize and close the door.

Kennedy was too quick for him. His foot was already in the opening, and he met the downward plunge of the knife with an upward blow on the overseer's arm which sent the knife flying back into the darkness of the warehouse, while with the other hand he clutched the man's throat. Instantly the sailors with the ropes leaped forward, and

63

before he could even try to reach the pistol in his belt, they had the arms of the would-be pirate pinioned behind him.

Even in the gray darkness Philpott's face was terrible to see. Kennedy kept his strangle hold upon his throat, thus damming a flood of profanity at its source, or the woods would have rung with oaths.

"Now, then, ye black-hearted villain," said Kennedy, "I'll fill your mouth with something better than the things ye'd like to say. Who's got a handkerchief?"

"Her-r-e's mine," said Sandy promptly, and when he heard those Scotch "r's" rolling through the darkness it probably dawned on the overseer just who at least one of his captors was!

Kennedy fitted Sandy's handkerchief neatly over the prisoner's mouth and took away his pistol and handed it to Sandy, and then the three men lifted him bodily like a log of wood and carried him back into the warehouse. The darkness in the building was so dense it could almost be felt. The open door showed only a dull gray patch against the blackness, as, feeling their way cautiously with their heavy burden, the men moved slowly back into the depths of the cavern.

"I've br-rought tinder-r and flint and a candle, Mister-r Kennedy," came Sandy's voice from somewhere, "if ye think it safe to str-rike a light."

At the sound of Sandy's voice, the overseer writhed in his captor's grasp and gave a gurgle which threatened to boil over and flood the place with venom in spite of the handkerchief.

"There, there, me darlin'," crooned Kennedy, as he gave the helpless overseer a soothing pat, which sounded, as one of the sailors remarked, 'like the slap of a whale's fluke on a dock,' "lie still and go by-by like a good little boy, and don't forget to say your prayers! If ye don't drop off by yerself, we'll have to put ye to sleep! Papa's got an engagement with some gintlemen, and can't be disturbed. Light up, Mr. McNair. It's lucky ye brought the candle. This baby's afraid to go to sleep in the dark."

A guffaw from the other sailors at this sally was nipped in the bud by the Irishman. "Hold yere whist, ye danderin' idiots," he said fiercely, "and keep yer grins inside of ye, where they'll be doin' nobody any harm."

"Shut the door-r, Tom," said Sandy softly, "we are ahead of their game, but we can't be too ca-r-re-ful."

"Two of you b'ys step outside," said Kennedy. "Stand out of sight and watch for the company. They're quality, and mustn't be kept waitin'!"

Two of the men slipped out in response to this order, the doors were closed, and after a few unsuccessful attempts Sandy struck a light and lit the candle.

"Now where at all is the cradle?" said Kennedy, looking about as the candle threw a feeble gleam into the dark corners of the great room, and fell on the purple face and rolling eye-balls of the prisoner. "Somethin' snug and warm it should be, for he's a fractious child and needs soothin'!"

"Will this do?" said Tom, pointing to the empty rum hogshead that he had shown Archie that morning.

"The very thing!" murmured Kennedy, and at his command the men folded the wretched overseer's legs together and shoved him into the cask. Then the cask was set upright.

"Where's the cover, lad?" said Kennedy, and when Tom produced it, he gravely fitted it on the top of the cask.

"Won't he smother?" asked Sandy.

"There's a bung-hole to breathe through," said Kennedy, "and it will soften him up to stew in his own p'ison a bit, surely. If it's too lively he is, we'll just roll the barrel off the end of the dock!"

A smothered howl broke from the cask and was promptly answered by a thump from Kennedy.

"Kape quiet," he said, "or I'll stop up the bung-hole on you!"

A silence as dense as the darkness followed, and Kennedy turned to the two men with ropes. "Now we'll get ready for callers," he said complacently. "You two boys," to the men with the ropes, "stand here; and you, Tom, climb up on top o' this pile of lumber out of the way and be ready to answer the Mustee when he calls. You others stand by! Ye'll know well enough what to do whin the time comes. This'll be no such simple trick, I'm tellin' ye. Now, Mr. McNair, douse the glim, but kape the candle handy, though I think we'll scarce be needin' it. It'll not be long now before the birds'll be singin' to wake the dawn."

VII. PIRATES

To Tom, sitting atop of the lumber-pile with Sandy standing guard in front of him, the next few moments seemed at least a month long. Kennedy took his knife from his belt and, cutting a sliver for a

seam in the door, widened the crack into a lookout and to this applied his eye. Then they waited, with nothing but the heavy breathing of the men, the occasional snapping of a twig in the forest, or the lonely cry of the whip-poor-wills to break the silence. Once the howl of a distant wolf sent a shiver down Tom's spine. He wondered what Archie and Trix were doing. He wondered if Captain Pepperell would come at the right time. He even prayed fervently in the dark, and it is not improbable that Sandy prayed too.

At last there was a soft knock on the door, and one of the men outside whispered through the crack, "Ship off to starboard, nothing else in sight."

"All right! come in, then," said Kennedy. The door swung open, the two watchers slipped inside, and it closed softly after them.

The early dawn was now just beginning to creep over the world, and the dim light shone in dull gray streaks through the cracks between the boards of the warehouse. Tom slid along on his high perch, and found a knot-hole which commanded a view of the river and the dock stretching two hundred feet from the shore into the channel. As the pirate ship sailed like a shadow up the river, Kennedy gave news of her progress to the watchers in the dark.

"She's a captured merchantman from her shape," he said. "She's coming up with a fair wind and the current against her quiet as a lady. The deck's swarming with the vermin. Whist, now! Maybe you can hear the captain's orders."

They strained their ears to listen, but the pier was long, and they heard nothing but a low creaking sound as the ship at last sidled gently up against the dock.

"It's like the ghost of a ship, manned by shadows," whispered Kennedy. "I never heard such silence in me life! Ready, now, boys. They've got the lines ashore and are makin' fast. The Mustee's leapt from the deck rail and is comin' up the dock as still as a black cat after the cream jug. Whist, now, all of you, and stand by."

They had but an instant to wait before the low owl cry sounded just outside the warehouse. Three times it quivered through the silent woods, and then the great door swung slowly and silently open and the black figure of the Mustee stood silhouetted against the gray of the early dawn. He crouched forward and peered into the blackness of the warehouse.

"Whar is you, Massa Philpott?" came his voice in a hoarse whisper, and Kennedy whispered back, "Here, step right in."

The Mustee took a step forward and instantly his windpipe was clutched in a grip of steel and he was dragged into the darkness by unseen hands. Like a serpent pinned to the ground by a forked stick, he writhed and twisted in the grasp of his captors, making strange strangling noises in his throat. Kennedy shook him as a terrier shakes a rat.

"Kape whist now, ye onprincipled old impostor," he muttered, bumping his victim's head on the floor, "tryin' for to pass yerself off for an owl! Another noise out of ye, and it's still enough ye'll be after it — and that I promise ye."

The two sailors had already taken away his pistol and cutlass and laid them on the lumber-pile beside Tom, and they now proceeded to gag the Mustee and tie him with ropes as they had already tied the overseer. This done, they carried him back into the corner of the warehouse and dumped him on the pile of pelts, and in less time than it takes to tell it were back at the door beside Kennedy.

The pirate ship was now securely made fast to the dock, and most of the crew were already ashore. On the poop deck the captain was giving final orders to some sailors who were in the rigging clewing up the topsail.

"Ready, boys!" said Kennedy in a low voice. "Line up here and kape back in the dark. Niver a sight of us can they see if we kape in the shadow, but only the open door waitin' for 'em. You, Tom, stay where ye are and when ye sight the Nunquam Dormio, sing out! We'll toll 'em along until Captain Pepperell comes up. If we start in on 'em too soon, they'll run back and get away with the ship. If we wait too long, they may see ours and run anyway." He looked anxiously at the brightening sky. "It'll be about four o'clock now, I'm thinkin'. The cocks are crowin'."

The pirates were now gathered in a knot on the dock, looking toward the warehouse and talking together in low tones.

"Why in blazes don't ye come on, ye leather-headed haythen?" muttered Kennedy.

"Maybe they're waiting for the signal," said Sandy.

Just then Tom gave a joyful bounce on his perch. "There she comes! there she comes! I see the Nunquam Dormio," he whispered.

"It's now or never, boys," said Kennedy. "Give 'em the call, Tom." Instantly the wild owl cry echoed through the woods.

69

The effect was magical. The pirates had evidently been waiting for it, and at once they swarmed silently up the dock like ants attacking a sugar-barrel. Nearer and nearer came the buccaneers, treading stealthily on the loose boards of the dock. Tom counted them. There were twenty great bearded, savage-looking ruffians, all armed with pistols and cutlasses, and he felt his hair slowly rising on his scalp as they approached.

"Steady, boys, steady! Kape back in the dark and fire at the ground just forninst 'em, when I give the word," said Kennedy in a husky whisper, and the seven men stood silent and alert with pistols loaded and ready.

The pirates reached the shore line before Kennedy shouted, "Give it to 'em, boys," and instantly the seven pistols spit seven bullets at the advancing thieves. There was a blood-curdling yell from the surprised buccaneers, and one who had been a little in advance of the others threw up his hands and fell forward on the dock. The next man behind him stumbled over his prostrate body and landed on top of him. Without a moment's delay the seven pistols spoke again, tearing up the earth about the now stampeded pirates, covering them with flying dirt and adding to their mad confusion.

"Back to the ship! back to the ship!" yelled the man who seemed to be in command of the party. "That devil of a Mustee has betrayed us! Run! run for your lives!"

Howling like wolves, the men turned their backs on the warehouse in a mad scramble to reach the ship. The men who had fallen struggled to their feet and fled with the others. The pirate captain, still on the deck, instantly began shouting orders to the few sailors on board and to those on shore.

"Cast off, cast off, you lubbers," he shrieked. "Man the yards! Put on every stitch of canvas."

The men flew in a desperate attempt to obey orders and get the ship away, but, just as they neared the end of the dock and sprang to the ropes, a volley from the Nunquam Dormio swept across the dock, cutting away the gang-plank.

"Kape quiet, boys!" shouted Kennedy. "He's got 'em marooned ashore, thanks be to God! Lave 'em to the Captain until they turn back this way, and kape yourselves back! If they see there are but seven of us, they'll rush the warehouse."

Caught between two fires, the distracted pirates ran first one way, then the other, and Tom, watching from his knot-hole, saw the Nunquam Dormio bearing steadily down-stream toward the dock, her guns firing volley after volley as she came.

"There she comes, the darlin'," shouted Kennedy, dancing with excitement as he watched their own ship sailing like a great bird of prey toward the helpless pirate craft. "It's Captain Pepperell'll teach you manners, you rascals! Go it, — go it like blazes, Cap'n! Speak your piece!"

As if in answer to his prayer the guns of the Nunquam Dormio sent another shot rattling through the rigging, and then to their great surprise there came an answering volley from the guns of the pirate ship.

"She can't keep that up," remarked Sandy, "most of the crew are ashore."

"And they'll stay ashore," growled another of the sailors, "unless they can fly."

Every eye in the warehouse was now fixed on the wild struggle at the end of the dock. The pirates were running distractedly to and fro, driven back every time they attempted to reach their ship, by cross fire from the Nunquam Dormio, and whenever they turned in the other direction by a volley from the warehouse.

It was now almost day. The eastern sky was ablaze with the colors of the dawn, and mockingbirds and cardinals were singing as though there were no such things as pirates in a happy world.

Meanwhile the Mustee, quite forgotten in the excitement, was struggling in his corner to free himself from the ropes which bound him. Lithe as a serpent, he twisted and turned until he had writhed one hand free, and with this he was able to remove the gag from his mouth and undo the other knots. Then he rolled quietly off the heap of pelts upon which he had been thrown, and in so doing bumped against the cask in which, unknown to him, the overseer was imprisoned. Philpott, meanwhile, had been bracing his back and knees and rocking back and forth in the only motion possible to him inside the cask, hoping to overturn it or burst it open. The sudden force of the Mustee's weight, added to his own efforts from inside sent the cask over, the cover rolled off, and the amazed half-breed found himself gazing in the dim light at the purple face of his companion in crime.

Though the cask made a noise in falling, the men at the warehouse door were so intent on the battle outside that none of them heard it. Silently the Mustee removed Sandy's handkerchief from the overseer's mouth and undid knots in the rope which bound him, and the two desperate men held a whispered conference. Then they crept silently forward on their hands and knees toward the door.

A moment later Tom, turning suddenly from his knot-hole, saw the Mustee's long, brown arm steal over the edge of the lumber-pile, and his lean brown hand seize the pistol which still lay beside him, while the other hand groped for the knife. Quick as a flash Tom seized the knife himself, and, lifting it high in the air, brought it down with all his force on the Mustee's groping hand. There was a sudden shriek of pain and rage from behind the lumber-pile, the hand was torn away, and a bullet from the Mustee's pistol grazed Tom's shoulder and buried itself in the rafters over his head.

Instantly every man at the door whirled about, and Kennedy found himself face to face with the overseer, who had found his knife on the floor and was poised to spring upon him and bury it in his back. The attack was well timed, for the men were in the act of reloading their pistols when the Mustee yelled. With the swift motion of a cat, Kennedy sprang aside as the overseer lunged forward, and, seizing the muzzle end of his empty pistol, brought the butt down on his head with 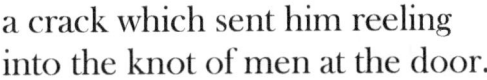 a crack which sent him reeling into the knot of men at the door.

Sandy, meanwhile, the moment the Mustee's shot was fired, had leaped to the lumber-pile beside Tom. "Ar-r-e ye hur-r-t?" he gasped.

"No," shouted Tom, pointing with the bloody knife at the Mustee on the floor behind the lumber-pile. The wretch was helpless for the moment, as his pistol was empty and reloading was difficult with his wounded hand.

Sandy at once began reloading his own pistol, but in the instant that it took the Mustee had crawled around the end of the lumber-pile on his hands and knees, and, charging head first like a bull into the group at the door, managed to upset two of the men.

In the wild confusion that followed, though both were wounded, he and overseer succeeded in breaking away from their captors, and, dashing down the dock, joined in the wild efforts of the marooned pirates to get back aboard their boat.

Here a new surprise awaited them, for the pirates turned furiously upon them, and shouting, "You betrayed us, you devils!" They hurled the two men from the dock into the channel, and they were seen no more.

As Sandy had prophesied, the return fire of the pirate ship was short-lived. Its situation was now desperate. Most of the crew were ashore, and the few on the vessel were either treed in the rigging or struggling with the guns. It was out of the question to get the ship under way with no crew, and as the Nunquam Dormio came swiftly downstream headed directly toward her, firing as she came, the pirate captain ran up a white flag with his own hands. The moment he had done so the firing ceased, the men in the rigging slid down the ropes in a hurry, and, running to the deck rail, leaped over the vessel's side and landed among the mob on the dock. Last of all, the Captain leaped too, and not risking the fate they knew they deserved in case they were captured, the pirates swarmed over the side of the dock at the water's edge and ran as fast as legs could carry them into the woods east of the warehouse, taking nothing with them but their weapons.

As the last man leaped to the ground and disappeared among the trees, the little army hidden in the warehouse burst from its hiding-place and dashed pell-mell down the dock to greet the Nunquam Dormio, which was now sliding up close alongside the abandoned vessel. Tom, dancing for joy, was several steps ahead of the others, with Sandy close behind, when a shout from Kennedy stopped them.

"Stop where ye are, ye dunderheads!" he cried. "Are ye thinkin' that just because they're out of sight those devils have no more fight left in them? They'll turn the trick on us yet if we aren't watchful. Sandy, go up on the roof and kape a lookout! It's nothing but short range weapons they have, so they'll need to come close if they attack us. Let you not be caught napping!"

Sandy at once ran back to the warehouse and, climbing on the lean-to, scrambled up where he could look over the ridge-pole of the roof and command a view of the woods and shore-line to the east and south. The other men were stationed as lookouts about the warehouse and on the dock, and Tom ran to the end of the pier to get the Captain's orders.

The Nunquam Dormio was now close beside the other ship. Captain Pepperell was standing on the poop deck; sailors were already in the rigging taking in canvas, and others were standing ready with lines to make her fast to the pirate ship.

"Board her, Kennedy, and take the ropes," shouted the Captain, and instantly Kennedy gave a running jump across the space where the gang-plank had been, and landed safely on deck, leaving Tom standing alone on the dock.

Dashing from bow to stern, Kennedy caught the ropes and tied the two ships securely together. Planks were laid from one to the other, and from the pirate ship to the dock and the next moment Tom, Archie, and Trix swarmed boldly over them from opposite sides and met on the deck.

"Not too fast," shouted Captain Pepperell, warningly. "We don't know yet that some of these varmints may not be hiding below decks. Kennedy, search the ship."

"Aye, aye, sir," said Kennedy, and, taking his pistol in hand, he went below immediately, followed by two sailors detailed by the Captain to go with him. While they were gone, Captain Pepperell took a survey of the deck to see how much damage had been done by the guns, and the three children retired to a safe spot in the end of the bow to talk it over.

"Oh, Tom, were you hurt?" asked Trix, the moment they were by themselves.

"Not exactly," said Tom, "but I almost was," and he displayed the bullet-hole in his sleeve with justifiable pride. "The Mustee did his best to finish me, but I did more to him than he did to me," he explained with satisfaction.

Trix examined his coat in a spasm of anxiety and affection. "Are you sure, Tom? There's blood on your cuff!" she said.

"It's his blood, not mine," Tom insisted stoutly, and then he told them the story of the fight in the warehouse.

Trix beamed with pride and shuddered with horror at the recital, and Archie gazed at Tom with something like envy. "It wasn't so exciting on the ship," he said regretfully. "I wish I'd been with you. The Captain made us go below when the firing began, and all we could do was to peep through the port-holes, but we saw it all."

Captain Pepperell was stooping over a small boat on the deck, when Kennedy and the two sailors came up the companion-way and appeared before him.

"All clear below, sir," said Kennedy. "We've been over her from stern to stern. It was a clean sweep ye made, Captain, and it's a handsome prize to take back to Boston. The hold is full of loot."

"I've been trying to make out her name," said the Captain, "but they've painted it out with black paint, on the life boats, as well as on the bow. She can't have been long in their hands, for they haven't put another name over it, and the black paint looks quite new. Perhaps we can find the ship's log when we go through her, but that will have to wait. It's been a hard night's work and it's time we had something to eat. Tell the cook to make coffee for all hands and feed us on deck."

"Aye, aye, sir," said Kennedy, and at once he ran over the connecting plank to the Nunquam Dormio with the Captain's orders.

In a little while the smell of coffee floated up from the cook's galley, and all hands were piped on deck for a sailor's breakfast of hard-tack and coffee as strong as lye.

"Keep your pistols and cutlasses handy," ordered the Captain as the men swarmed over the pirate ship and found places for themselves on the two decks. "Kennedy, keep a sharp lookout and have the ship's guns ready. If the varmints come back, we'll turn their own guns on them."

"Aye, aye, sir," said Kennedy, "but what about feeding *them?*" he asked pointing to the figure of Sandy still glued to the roof of the warehouse and to the other men on guard.

"Let me take some coffee to them," said Archie, springing forward.

"Me, too, sir," said Tom, following suit.

The Captain nodded. The ship's boy brought a bucket of coffee and some mugs, and the two lads hastened with this and the hard-tack to the tired men at the warehouse. A few moments later Trix, enthroned beside the Captain, and sharing his breakfast, was thrilled by the sight of Mr. Alexander McNair sitting calmly astride the ridge-pole with a pistol in front of him, a mug in one hand and a ship's biscuit in the other, eating his breakfast as serenely as if this extraordinary arrangement were his daily habit.

VIII. AUNT CYNTHIA TO THE RESCUE!

As soon as the hasty breakfast was eaten, the Captain called the scattered crew together on the deck of the pirate ship.

"Men," said he, "you've done this night's work well, but the job isn't finished yet. There's little food or rest for any one until the cargo from the warehouse is safely stowed below decks on the Nunquam Dormio and we are off for Boston with the pirate ship under convoy. It will leave both ships short-handed to divide the crew, but by keeping near together we shall make out to get them safe to port, I have no doubt, and then you'll get your prize money. Mr. Kennedy, you are to be the master of the prize. Pick out your crew, cast off our lines, and take your ship to the pier at Honeywood. Make her fast there, leave one man aboard on watch, and bring the rest back on foot as soon as you can. Meanwhile, we'll warp the Nunquam Dormio to this dock and get the goods aboard."

The Captain's speech was greeted with cheers, and the men set to work with a will to carry out his orders. Kennedy, flushed with pride at his new honors, called out the five men who had been with him in the warehouse, and four others. New men were placed on guard duty ashore, and the work of getting the pirate ship out of the way began.

The children, meanwhile, had been sitting in a row on the roof of the Captain's cabin on the Nunquam Dormio. Captain Pepperell turned to them.

"Now, my hearties," he said smiling, "you've certainly made a proud record for yourselves by this night's work, but in my opinion you'd better get back to Honeywood as soon as you can. It's full sun-up, and your aunt will be frantic with anxiety if she finds your beds empty. Call Mr. McNair down from the roof and get along with you."

"Aye, aye, sir!" said the three, and though they wanted very much to stay, they tumbled off their perch at once and obeyed orders like good seamen, and soon were on their way up the home trail with Sandy.

It was a glorious bright morning. The dew sparkled like diamonds on every leaf; the air was alive with bird-songs and the flutter of wings, and the slaves, whose day began at sunrise and ended at sundown, were already on their way to the field, when the four tired adventurers came out of the woods and saw the sun shining on the white portico of Honeywood. Astonishment was written on every black face as the toilers saw the children and Sandy McNair coming up the cart-path by the tobacco-field at that hour in the morning. Usually no one was astir in the big house until the workers had been in the fields for several hours.

"What shall we say to them?" said Trix to Sandy. "They'll wonder why the overseer isn't about and we'll have to tell them something."

"We mustn't let them know old Pillbox isn't coming back," said Tom. "They wouldn't do a lick of work if we did. We'll have to keep it from them until Father gets back anyway."

"But how can we? They'll see he isn't here," protested Trix.

They overtook Mammy Jinny, who was on her way from her cabin to the kitchen. She stopped short as she saw the children and their tutor.

"Fo' de Lawd sake, whar yo' all been at dis yer onrageous hour?" she demanded, looking at them in astonishment. "Yo' all look like you jus' been dug up!"

"We've been down to see Captain Pepperell's boat come in," said Trix quickly. "They are loading her now."

Even this plausible explanation failed to satisfy Mammy. She looked them over with suspicion. They were dirty and disheveled, and even Mr. Alexander McNair showed unmistakable signs of having been out all night.

"It suttinly pears tuh me like they's mighty queer gwines on on dis yer plantation," she grumbled. "I lay you chilluns is up to some debilment. Las' night yo' all sparkin' roun' in de big woods ontwel long atter sundown, an' los' de snack I don' fix fer ye, basket 'n' all — an' now here you is comin' along de track de yuther way at sun-up! You sho'ly is bleeged to be as empty as a rain-bar'l in a dry spell. Come 'long o' me, the whole bilin' of you, ontwel I rastle up a brekfus fer you."

"But Mammy, we've had our breakfast already," said Trix.

"Whar yo' all been to git brekfus while de cock's crowin' fer sun-up? You jus' splanify dat," demanded Mammy.

"On Captain Pepperell's ship," Trix answered.

"Humph," Mammy grunted contemptuously. "Sailor-man's vittles! You go 'long to de big house, honey, and w'en Mammy sends in some o' dem sassingers and co'n bread, I reckon yo' appetite'll rise up." Saying this, she turned off to the kitchen.

It was still early when they reached the big house. Mr. McNair and the two boys let themselves into the school-house with his key, and Trix went in by way of the kitchen and the corridor and crept quietly up to her room. For a moment it looked as if the adventure of the night, for a little while at least, might pass unnoticed, but just as she had her hand on the door-knob of her own room she heard Aunt Cynthia's voice, and Aunt Cynthia herself in dressing-gown and slippers with her hair still in curl-papers appeared suddenly in her doorway.

"Becky," she called, but Becky was not there, and then she caught sight of Trix standing fully dressed at the door of her room.

"Beatrix Burwell!" she cried, looking her over. "What on earth have you been doing out at this hour? Your shoes are all wet with dew, and you look as if you had been up all night!" She swept by her, looked into her room at the untouched bed, and stopped short. She opened her mouth, but no words came. Beatrix, meanwhile, was hastily getting her wits together in an effort to break the news of the night's adventure in the best possible way.

"But, Auntie," she began, and then, chancing to glance out the window, she saw the pirate ship just tying up to the pier in front of the house! If offered a welcome distraction. "Look, look!" she cried pointing to it.

Aunt Cynthia looked. "What in the world — what — what —" she began and then words failed her. "That isn't Captain Pepperell's ship! Beatrix Burwell, what's been going on here since I went to bed yesterday?"

"Well, Auntie, you see," began Beatrix desperately, "that isn't the Nunquam Dormio. It's a pirate ship."

At the word "pirate" Aunt Cynthia threw up her hands. "Pirates!" gasped the poor lady, sinking into a chair. "What shall we do? Where's Philpott? Where's Mr. McNair? Where are the boys?"

"There, there, Auntie, it's all right," said Trix, trying her best to soothe her, but not getting on well with explanations. "You see old Philpott is a pirate himself, or at least he meant to be one."

This additional crumb of information made the curl-papers fairly tremble, and at that very moment, the pirate ship having been made fast to the pier, they saw Kennedy and seven men file over the gang-plank and start toward the house.

"See them, see them!" cried Aunt Cynthia. "They are coming to attack the house! We shall all be murdered!"

In the instant of what she thought to be extreme danger all her fears seemed to vanish. She rose from her chair in spite of Beatrix's frantic efforts to explain, swept her into her room, and locked the door on her.

"Stay there," she commanded, "where you will be safe. I will meet the wretches myself."

In vain Beatrix pounded on the door and poured a flood of explanation and protests through the keyhole. She might just as well have tried to stop the rain from falling or the wind from blowing. Aunt Cynthia did not even hear her. The Burwell blood was up, and she was hurrying down-stairs with the desperate intention of defending the house herself with one of the muskets which hung on the wall of the great hall.

Beatrix heard her calling, "Becky — Mammy — Pam — come here quick! Ring the big bell! Call Mr. McNair!" and then she could distinguish nothing more, for the confused sound of banging doors and hurrying feet and the clanging of the plantation bell drowned out her aunt's martial tones.

In despair she hurried to the window, and, leaning far out, called, "Tom! Archie! Sandy!"

The heads of her brother and cousin immediately appeared at the windows opposite. "Oh, boys," she cried, "run quick! Aunt Cynthia has locked me in my room. She thinks Kennedy and the other sailors are pirates coming to attack the house, and she's going to meet them with a gun!"

The boys did not wait to reply, and Beatrix watched the next scene in the drama from her front window. She saw the men come up from the dock along the primrose-bordered path. She saw her intrepid aunt, her curl-papers bristling, go down the steps of the porch to meet them carrying her father's fowling-piece, and behind her, armed with a poker, came faithful Mammy Jinny. There was a sound as of other feet behind them, but the roof of the porch cut off her view.

Kennedy was in the lead of his men and, seeing a lady awaiting them, he gallantly saluted and Aunt Cynthia, at this pacific gesture, grounded arms and sternly awaited his approach. What would have happened had they really met each other just then will never be known, for at that moment Tom and Archie, followed by Sandy, dashed around the corner of the house and running forward, joined the group of men and came on with them toward the house. Trix saw Tom bring the men forward one by one and present them to his astonished and bewildered aunt, in his very best manner, then she collapsed on her bed in a fit of hysterical laughter.

"I always said Aunt Cynthia was no coward, if she is a lady," she gasped, "and Mammy Jinny! Bless her old heart — with her poker!" She laughed, and sobbed, and then, being utterly worn out, fell over on her pillow, and slept from sheer exhaustion.

IX. THE PIRATE SHIP

When she awoke an hour or two later she found her door open and the house as quiet as a church on Monday morning. She sprang up, and after a hasty toilet ran down to find out what was going on about the plantation. The boys and Sandy were nowhere to be seen, her aunt had disappeared entirely, and she went to the kitchen to get from Mammy an account of what had happened during her imprisonment in her room. She found her bending over the fire-place in the kitchen, where a great array of pots and pans was collected and the air was full of the smell of things cooking.

"You po' lil' lamb," cried Mammy when Trix appeared. "Yo' suttinly mus' be protracted along of all this yer rumpus! Set right down here, honey, and let Mammy git yo' a snack, and den yo' git along out o' here, 'case I'se mo' busier than a man killin' a snake."

"Where is everybody?" asked Trix, taking the great slice of cake which Mammy brought her and seating herself on the kitchen table to eat it.

"Well," said Mammy, "de boys went back to the warehouse wid dem pirates, which they ain't pirates at all but jus' Cap'n Pepperell's sailor-men. Can't keep no boy away fum de pot whar trouble's bilin'! They jus' boun' fer to mess up with it. An' Miss Cynthy she tuk and mount her hoss like the day o' jedgment, she did, an' rid off to the field, 'case de oberseer he ain't comin' back no mo', and Mars McNair he up and went along, to do the cussin', I reckon. They ridin' roun' de field now."

"What happened?" asked Trix. "I was locked in my room, so I couldn't hear a thing."

"Well, dey was a great splanification," said Mammy, "and yo' Auntie she say we boun' to have a big dinner and feed all dem sailors and the Captain and ev'ybody, and dey projeckin' a bobbycue out yander dis minute. Dey got de holes dug, and I spec from the squealin' I hearn a while back, de shoats is cookin' already. All the house niggers is fixin' vegetables and cleanin' chickens down by de washhouse and I'se cookin' 'em mo' stiddy than a horse trottin'."

Having finished her cake, Beatrix left the kitchen, and, passing the wash-house and the smoke-house, where groups of negroes were laughing and talking as they worked, stopped at the stables and ordered out her horse. In a moment more she was on Prince Charlie's back, flying down the cart-path toward the warehouse. Aunt Cynthia and Sandy were riding majestically along at the far end of the tobacco-field as she passed, but, not wishing to be stopped on her errand, she galloped by and pretended not to see them. She met Captain Pepperell and the boys coming back from the warehouse. The boys were leading their horses, and Beatrix wheeled Prince Charlie and fell in at the rear of the little procession.

"We're going over the pirate ship to see what we can find out about her, while Kennedy finishes the job at the warehouse," said the Captain. "I didn't want to stop for anything until I knew the cargo was safe. Those varmints can't do much harm now if they do come back. A pirate without a ship is as helpless as a turtle on its back. They'll make for the Carolina coast and join some other pirate crew, or I miss my guess. We won't take any chances, but I don't look for any further trouble from them."

Trix leaned from her saddle, and called in her most wheedling tone, "Captain, may *I* go over the pirate ship with you?"

"To be sure, to be sure!" said the Captain heartily. "Why not? Why not? Miss Cynthia too! And I am sorry your good father is not here to share in our discoveries."

At the tobacco-field they overtook Aunt Cynthia and Sandy, who were on the way home after finishing their tour of inspection, and, leaving the horses at the stable, all six went immediately to the pier and were ushered on board the pirate ship by the anchor watch.

Captain Pepperell at once led the way across the deck to the Captain's cabin. A scene of hopeless confusion met their eyes as the cabin door swung open. The bed was unmade, and the disordered bedding bore the marks of heavy boots. An empty keg smelling strongly of rum was overturned in the corner and empty mugs discolored with dregs littered the table and floor. The chart had been blown by the wind and wet with spray and hung in tattered shreds from the wall. The captain's sea chest stood open and empty, rifled of all its contents. They searched everywhere through the confusion for the log, but it was nowhere to be found.

"The villains threw it overboard more than likely, when they captured the vessel," said the Captain, grinding his teeth. "There's nothing to be learned here," and, leaving the captain's cabin, they went down the companion-way, and searched the ship from fo'csle to stern below decks. There was disorder everywhere — dirt and cockroaches. In the cook's galley they were greeted by a mess of dirty pots and pans and the smell of stale food, and a rat ran across the table before their very eyes.

It was here that Aunt Cynthia resigned. She gathered her ample skirts about her, lifting them lest they touch some unclean thing, and said to Beatrix: "Come with me, child. I am going back on deck. This is no place for a lady."

"Oh, but Auntie," pleaded Beatrix, "I've never been on a pirate ship before in my whole life. Maybe it's full of Spanish gold below, and even if I do get dirty, I can be washed, you know. Please let me!"

Aunt Cynthia sighed and rolled her eyes upward with a resigned expression. "Very well," said she, "but I wash my hands of it, and if you catch the plague it's no fault of mine!"

With this inspiring thought she went back on deck and sat down on a coil of rope with her skirts drawn close around her, and spent the next half-hour while the others were below in keeping a sharp lookout for more rats.

She was beginning to think the others were never coming back, when there was a bumping and scraping below decks as of heavy things being dragged about, and the Captain's voice called to the watch on deck, "Come below and lend a hand."

"Aye, aye, sir," cried the sailor, who at once disappeared down the companion-way, leaving Aunt Cynthia quite alone. In a few moments, flushed and beaming, Beatrix appeared before her

"Oh, Auntie," she cried, "what do you think we've found? What *do* you think we've found? It's Archie's mother's portrait and all the silver and things that were sent over in the Raleigh! They were all boxed up and lying on top of everything else in the hold. Archie recognized them at once, for he was there when they were packed, and there was Father's name marked on them as plain as day — Major George Burwell, Honeywood, Virginia! Oh, Auntie, isn't it wonderful?" and, forgetting in her joyous excitement all about the proprieties, Beatrix flung her arms about her aunt's neck and nearly unseated her from her coil of rope.

"Charlotte's portrait? Where?" cried Aunt Cynthia.

"They're bringing it," said Beatrix, dancing to the companion-way, and a moment later the corner of a big box appeared above the deck-level. Box after box was brought up and placed before her, until Aunt Cynthia was almost hidden behind the barricade.

"They were on top of everything else," said the Captain, "which shows the Raleigh must have been the last ship that fell into their clutches. The hold is full of stolen merchandise which cannot be opened until we get our prize to port."

He sighed heavily as he thought of the Raleigh — perhaps lying at that moment at the bottom of the sea, or else wrecked on some unknown coast, and being beaten to pieces by the waves. He thought, too, of her gallant captain and crew, possibly drowned or marooned on some uninhabited island, and no doubt he wondered if this fate awaited his own brave ship as well.

But the Captain was not one to spend time in mourning over what could not be helped, so he gave himself a little shake and said to Aunt Cynthia, "I'd like to get the goods for Honeywood ashore as soon as possible and my men are all busy at the warehouse."

"Tom, call Sam and Jo and any of the field hands you can get hold of," said Aunt Cynthia, and Tom disappeared at once on this errand.

The boxes were soon carried to the great hall, and first of all the case containing the portrait of Archie's mother was opened. The children and Aunt Cynthia watched eagerly as wrapping after wrapping was unfolded, and the painting was at last revealed. It showed a lovely lady, a little resembling Aunt Cynthia but not so severe, seated on a garden bench with a dog beside her. In the background, beyond some trees, appeared the towers of a castle.

"That's Kenmore," said Archie proudly, "and that's my dog beside Mother."

They looked at the lovely face for some time in silence, and then, by Aunt Cynthia's orders, the picture was hung above the fire-place in the dining-room at Honeywood, where it hangs to this day, smiling down on the present generation of Burwells as it smiled on the three children and Aunt Cynthia that day so long ago.

X. "GOOD-BY, FARE YOU WELL"

The hours of the exciting day flew by as if on wings. By two o'clock the warehouse was empty and locked, and by three the Nunquam Dormio lay serenely anchored in the channel just off the Honeywood pier. Captain Pepperell and his men were all ashore except those left to guard the ships, and in the field beyond the stables the smoke of the

barbecue curled upward from the pits, where whole pigs were roasting. A steady stream of slaves bore from the kitchen steaming dishes of fried chicken and potatoes and onions and cabbage and every other good thing which the season afforded, to the hungry sailors seated in groups under the trees and eating as if each individual man housed a whole famine in his own insides.

Such smells as there were! They floated out over the water to the unfortunate men on shipboard who had to stand watch while the others ate, and drove them nearly distracted. By and by their turn came, too, and by nightfall there was not a white person on the whole plantation who had not celebrated the defeat of the pirate by eating himself chock-full. Even the slaves were given a special allowance of corn-meal and permission to have a barbecue of their own after sundown when they came in from their day's works in the fields.

The longest day must come to an end, and at last the children were sent to their beds, the Captain returned to his ship, the lights in the big house went out one by one, and Honeywood slept in the moonlight as quietly as if no danger had ever threatened her peace.

News of the disappearance of Adam Philpott had spread among the negroes, from the sailors, and long after the big house was quiet a great bonfire still blazed before the cabins in the quarters, throwing strange, wild shadows across the fields as the slaves celebrated their deliverance from the hated overseer by weird dances and their own plaintive songs.

The next day passed, and the next, and still there was no news of Major Burwell. It seemed that the sudden fear of the pirates had passed only to give place to steady, long-continued dread of the Indians and fear lest the Major might never return from his dangerous mission across the river. Aunt Cynthia strove valiantly to keep the negroes at their work, and Sandy helped her in every way he could. The children tried to apply themselves to their lessons, but after such exciting events and because of the suspense about their father, the days dragged.

The Captain had taken the Nunquam Dormio back up the river again to collect the cargoes and commissions which he had been obliged to leave behind when he answered the children's call for help. Mr. Kennedy with a few sailors stayed with the pirate ship at the pier to repair damages and get her ready to join the Captain when he came back down the river. It was on Monday that the Nunquam Dormio had first appeared at Honeywood. It was now Saturday, and still no news had come from the Major. The children had finished their lessons and were perched on the deck rail of the pirate ship watching Kennedy splice a rope, when Archie suddenly leaped to his feet shouting, "There she comes!" and there, indeed, was the Nunquam Dormio coming swiftly down the river, the current and the breeze both with her!

In the prow, looking eagerly shoreward stood a man, and as the ship came nearer, Tom's quick eye was first to discover and his quick tongue the first to shout, "It's Father! it's Father!"

Such a scurrying about as there was then! The children raced back to the house to tell Aunt Cynthia and Sandy, and when half an hour later the Nunquam Dormio came skimming along over the waters and anchored in the channel, nearly all Honeywood was gathered on the pier to welcome the Major home.

He came ashore in the small boat with the Captain, and while the Captain conferred with Kennedy and inspected the pirate ship to see if she was ready for the homeward voyage, the Major told them how the Indians had been defeated and scattered and he, returning, had found the Captain at the Westover dock and had learned from him the story of the week at Honeywood. He said little to the children then. Later, when he had seen the portrait of his sister, and the boxes rescued from the pirate ship, and had visited the empty warehouse, he stood with them for a moment before the mantel in the drawing-room, meaning to give them the praise they deserved.

He looked first at the motto, "*Virtus omnia vincit*," then he looked at the children, and, just because he was so proud of their courage which had conquered so much, he choked and couldn't say anything at all! He hugged them instead, — all three at once, — and they understood what he would have liked to say and were happy.

That afternoon, as the shadows were lengthening across the fields, the family assembled once more on the pier to say good-by to Captain Pepperell. Kennedy with his crew on board the prize ship, and the other crew waited in the channel for the Captain's return.

"Call all hands and get ready for sea," shouted the Captain as he came down the pier with the Major.

The sailors sprang to obey. Hot coffee was served to all hands on both decks. Then the pirate ship moved majestically away from the dock.

The Captain watched her as she swung slowly out into the channel, then he said good-by and sprang into the waiting small boat, and soon they saw him climb the Jacob's ladder up the side of the

Nunquam Dormio and disappear over the rail. The sailor followed him, and then the small boat itself was hauled up out of sight. From over the water they heard the Captain's voice, "Man the windlass, and break out the anchor." Again came the creaking of the windlass, and a sailor's song floated shoreward —

> *"O, blow, my boys,*
> *I long to hear you,*
> *Blow, boys, blow.*
> *O, blow, my boys,*
> *I long to hear you,*
> *Blow, my bully boys, blow."*

From the deck of the pirate ship sailors' voices sent back an answering strain —

> *"There's a pirate ship*
> *Coming down the river,*
> *Blow, boys, blow,*
> *Every roll her tops'ls shiver,*
> *Blow, my bully boys, blow."*

Then came a roar from the Nunquam Dormio —

> *"And who do you think*
> *She has for Captain?*
> *Blow, boys, blow.*
> *Cap'n Pepp'rell, that fine old sailor,*
> *Blow, my bully boys, blow."*

As if the singing voices were their very own, the two ships moved slowly down-stream with the level rays of the sun gilding their white sails, until they looked like great yellow moths on the dark waters of the James. Fainter and fainter sounded the music, smaller and smaller grew the sails, until a bend in the shore-line hid them altogether from the watchers on the pier.

Then the Major and Aunt Cynthia returned to the big house, Mr. McNair went back to the school-room, and the children, left to themselves, wandered on down the river-bank to the Big Oak.

As they reached it and prepared to climb to the tree house, Beatrix heaved a great sigh of relief. "I've had all the adventures I want," she said, "and I hope nothing will happen at Honeywood for a long, long time," and Archie, swinging himself up into the tree, perched like a bird on one of the lower limbs long enough to sing Ariel's song,

"Merrily, merrily shall we live now
Under the blossom that hangs on the bough."

Published by

Bluewater Publications is a multi-faceted publishing company capable of meeting all of your reading and publishing needs. Our twofold aim is to:

1) Provide the market with educationally enlightening and inspiring research and reading materials
2) Make the opportunity of being published available to any author or researcher who desires to become published

We are passionate about preserving history; whether it is through the republishing of an out-of-print classic or by publishing the research of historians and genealogists, Bluewater Publications is the publisher you need.

To learn more about the person who wrote this book or for information about how you can be published through Bluewater Publications, please visit:

www.BluewaterPublications.com

Confidently Preserving Our Past,
Bluewater Publications.com
Formerly Known as Heart of Dixie Publishing

www.ingramcontent.com/pod-product-compliance
Lightning Source LLC
Chambersburg PA
CBHW080544180626
46818CB00008B/3118